Lisa Foxall was born in 1983 in South Devon, England. From a young age she enjoyed writing short stories and novels, but never published any of her work. This book is her first attempt at publication. Her writing style is influenced by classic authors ranging from Emily Brontë to Bram Stoker, whose books she eagerly read growing up.

To both my grandparents, Les and Edna Barr. Also, to William and Pamla Foxall. I love you all and miss you very much.

Lisa Foxall

THE BRUMMIE BOYS OF ASTON

AUSTIN MACAULEY PUBLISHERS™
LONDON · CAMBRIDGE · NEW YORK · SHARJAH

Copyright © Lisa Foxall 2024

The right of Lisa Foxall to be identified as the author of this work has been asserted by the author in accordance with Sections 77 and 78 of the Copyright, Designs and Patents Act 1988.

All rights reserved. No part of this publication may be reproduced, stored in a retrieval system, or transmitted in any form or by any means, electronic, mechanical, photocopying, recording, or otherwise, without the prior permission of the publishers.

Any person who commits any unauthorised act in relation to this publication may be liable to criminal prosecution and civil claims for damages.

This is a work of fiction. Names, characters, businesses, places, events, locales, and incidents are either the products of the author's imagination or used in a fictitious manner. Any resemblance to actual persons, living or dead, or actual events is purely coincidental.

A CIP catalogue record for this title is available from the British Library.

ISBN 9781035812479 (Paperback)
ISBN 9781035812486 (ePub e-book)

www.austinmacauley.co.uk

First Published 2024
Austin Macauley Publishers Ltd®
1 Canada Square
Canary Wharf
London
E14 5AA

Thanks to my publisher for believing in my first novel and for taking a risk on a first-time author.

Part 1

Chapter 1
Witton Road
Birmingham 1993

Making their way to the local pub, all four friends blind drunk bellowed, screamed and smashed everything they saw.

Out of the four, David and Thomas seemed to be the worse for sure. Ernest and Henry seemed to be halfway there.

"For fuck's sake, walk fucking straight!"

Henry pushed David to one side as he walked like a drunken scarecrow that had been tied up for too long.

"Don't fucking push me. I mean it!"

Slurring his words and wiping his mouth, David's hat was too forward almost covering his eyes.

"If I wanted to push you, I would do it down a flight of stairs," threatening David as they begin to walk slower.

"You having a fuckin' go?"

The two young men stopped dead in the middle of a quite black and cold night. The street lights were all that was used for light. Only the grey moon showed when the black clouds did not cover it.

Face-to-face, the pair squared up to each other, one unable to fight. The other would happily put the other in the hospital.

"Come on leave it, yeah?"

Ernest broke in between them for fear of the cops being called.

"Yes, just leave each other alone. Off to the pub!"

Thomas voluntarily called. David walked on ahead. Henry for lord. As they continued, a voice was coming from beside him.

"OI!"

Ernest had picked up a bicycle that belonged to the local baker's shop.

"Want a ride?"

Ernest asked as Henry looked at it.

"Go on. I'll get on the back."

Henry climbed up, and the pair drifted away.

Thomas laughed while David told him his legs were not working properly.

"Wooo!"

Ernest and Henry screamed out in laughter as they rode off down the road filled with fun. The streets had become their playground, and no one could put a stop to their way of play.

"Ernest... Corner!"

The bicycle's front wheel wobbled from side to side causing it to swirl and hit the edge of the pavement. Crashing down fast and hard, it caused the local shoemaker to wake. His bedroom light went on, and he opened his window to see what was going on at such a late hour.

"You lot! Don't you know what the time it is?"

"Some of us have to sleep!"

Thomas looked up with a filthy look on his unshaven face and stuck his middle finger up at the man.

Insulted by such a gesture, the man closed the window, and the light went out.

"Bastard."

"Yeah."

Thomas turned very slowly so as not to fall over.

"What?"

"What?"

David looked as though he was about to wet himself the way he was walking.

"You alright, our kids?" Thomas asked the young men.

"Yeah. We are. But the bikes are not."

As they strolled from around the corner, Ernest was pushing the damaged bike. Its wheels got spiked, and the back wheel nearly came off.

"So? What are you going to do with that?"

David very slowly and carefully asked as Henry looked at Ernest.

"Leave it."

"OK," shrugging his shoulders Ernest released his hands from the handles. The bike hit the road hard and loudly.

"TO THE … INN … PUB!" Thomas ordered like an officer pointing down the road. The others looked and followed not knowing they were being watched.

A beautiful, dark-skinned woman was watching them as they walked past her house.

Bella was tall and had dark hair and brown eyes, and she got a figure that was shaped like an hourglass. No one could understand why such a beautiful woman would be in a 'relationship' with Thomas, a man in his late thirties but looked older, unshaven and drunk most times. Yet she loved him and worried about him, even more since he came back from the Falklands War.

Staring out the window and watching them disappear around the corner, Bella closed the curtain, walked across the cold bedroom floor and crawled into bed saying, "No point in keeping his side warm; he'll pass out in the living room again."

The whole place was built with smoked, dark wooden tables and chairs that had a dark green colour that made the place feel a bit closed in. The thick heavy door swung open slamming the back of the long church-like chair, where a group of young wild women were sitting drinking like goldfish and fags in between their dirty fingers.

Entering the pub, Ernest and Henry stumbled towards the back table to put Thomas down. Their heavy weight on the two young men went slowly, and without knocking anything, they made them sit down quickly and quietly.

"Here, Ernest, drop 'em here."

Henry sat Thomas upright, but through gritted teeth, David fell down and began to snooze.

The pub was now half empty as the night drew to an end, and those still inside showed no signs of leaving anytime soon.

"I'll get 'em, and what do you want?" Henry asked in a smoky voice as he took out his money from his biker, black jacket pocket.

"I'll have the same again and a small whiskey," Thomas whispered as he placed his arms on the table barely able to talk.

"Ernest?"

"I'll have a small Shandy."

Henry looked a bit surprised not something Ernest what normally ask for.

"What? One of us has to stay sober to get us home."

Turning to look at a passed-out David, Henry was going to get him one in case. He suddenly woke up.

"I'll pay you back, our kid."

Thomas slurred his words as he leaned forward.

"You already did."

Henry pulled out Thomas's wallet from his coat pocket. He was in no state to fight back.

"Heyyy…"

Smiling, Henry walked over to the bar.

"OI!" the landlord, an old man with plump red face, called him from behind the bar pointing his finger at Henry who stopped just before getting to the bar.

"I don't want any trouble from you like the last time. When you were here before, you smashed the place up. It took me days and weeks to get everything replaced."

"Don't worry, George. Two out of four of us are too pissed to stand."

The landlord went over to him and finally got up to the sticky bar placing his left foot on the brass foot pole.

"Usual, please. And one small whisky."

Wiping the glasses with a tea towel, the landlord leaned a little while Henry counted his money.

"What are you doing tomorrow night at about seven o'clock?"

This was an opportunity to really worry the landlord as Henry looked up from his wallet. He had the bluest eyes anyone had seen.

"George, I din't know you cared."

"What? Oh fuck. No, I mean can you work tomorrow night?"

Henry unfolded his pocket of cigarette papers and made one to his fingers that was a sign that he was a chain smoker.

"Why?" he asked as he slipped the cigarette in between his thin lips.

"Our barmaid is off tomorrow to meet her boyfriend, and the other one can't fill in, so? How about it? I'll pay you. Cash in hand."

"Alright." Henry took his cigarette out the side of his mouth for a moment.

"Ten bob an hour."

"Ten bob! Piss off!"

"Fine."

"OK OK. Ten bob an hour. And mmm… Ernest?"

Henry turned silently to check that everything was alright.

"What about him?"

"Does he want to do some glass collecting tomorrow night?"

"Yeah, yeah, for ten Bob."

"You're taking the piss. I'll be fuckin' skint!"

No reply came from a lit-up Henry.

"Fine. Ten bob each. See you tomorrow night. At seven."

Taking the tray of drinks away, Henry gave a quick wink with his right eye and left the bar making his way to the table.

"Here you go."

"Tar."

Handing out the drinks, the pint glasses clinked, and David who was sleeping in the corner of the long sofa chair finally woke up.

"Oh, bitch."

No one answered as he finally come around.

"We're workin' tomorrow night. You're collecting glasses." Henry tapped Ernest's arm as he told him about the possibility of earning ten bob an hour, cash in hand.

"Where? Here?"

"Yes? Well, where else did you think?"

"How much again?"

"Ten bob an hour."

"Fine."

Handing out the drinks, Thomas knocked back a small whisky and slammed the empty glass onto the table.

"I'm going to the men's."

Henry turned to walk away as a red eye, David could not control himself to say some sort of remark.

"Going to get sucked!?"

Looking over his shoulder, Henry opened his arms and told him that he should not get so jealous. He could always join him. David collapsed back down on the chair. Henry gave a smile and made his way to the gent's toilet.

You hate the smell as soon as you walked through the door. Men who had missed their target, dripping off the edge of the urinals, towels all over the floor and sick down the back of the toilet inside the cubicle.

Undoing his trouser zip and standing there not noticing anyone, Henry heard the door open but did not notice for a moment.

"My… my… Haven't we got bigger?"

Looking up, Henry recognised that voice and finished himself off as quickly as possible.

"What do you want?"

The man was dressed in a grey suit and shoes to match. He got black, thin, long hair and a black moustache. As he walked closer, Henry could hear the heels of the man's shoes.

"Well, I have come to see if you are willing to come tonight?" The man's voice was rude.

"No, not tonight. I've got work tomorrow morning."

Henry, he did his trouser zip back up quickly and turned to wash his hands in a fashion of quick under a cold tap and then wiped them on the paper towel that set in a pile near the urinals.

"Fine. Tomorrow night?"

"Working here."

Henry leaned up against the sink. His head turned ever so slightly back. He gave a small smile.

"Oh, well. What about Ernest?"

The smile disappeared, and all Henry saw was red.

"What about Ernest?" "Is he?"

"No, he fucking isn't."

The man seemed somewhat shocked at Henry's anger. His change of attitude had never been touched.

"I'm warning you. If you touch him, I'll fucking cut it off."

Turning his heels, the man slowly walked away towards the door but not before looking back for a moment to blow a kiss to his old rent boy who turned to grab the bar of soap. The man quickly turned back and gave a smile.

"Sweet dreams."

Finally leaving the door closed shut, he returned back to the sink dropping the soap onto the floor, and placing his hands on either side of the sink, he closed his blue eyes as though he was going to throw up.

"He's been a while?"

Thomas began to wonder what was happening inside the toilet for fear that a fight might break out, and he was missing out on the action.

"I'll go and see what's wrong."

Getting up Ernest saw a man in the grey suit as he headed towards the toilets. Henry also came out.

"You were a while. I thought you'd fallen down."

Not hearing what Ernest was saying as he watched the man disappear out of the pub and casually stroll passed the window.

"Henry?"

"What?"

There was a moment of silence between the two as Henry continued to look out the window while Ernest was just looking at him.

"You alright?"

Facing Ernest, Henry shook his head and dropped his eyes before looking back at him.

"Yeah, yeah, yeah, I am fine. Come on; let's have every drink before George calls time."

Gently touching Ernest's back, the pair went to join their friends and finish their drinks.

The mist has started to roll in the dark blue sky. An ice-cold chill cut right through them as Henry and Ernest helped their friends back home near Witton Road.

Thomas was a heavyweight as Ernest had dragged him on his shoulders making him grind his teeth unable to balance him and without falling on himself.

Henry was just in front of him without David.

"Here, we'll drop this piss head off first."

Henry stopped as he shoved David against four-foot damp wall at the bottom of his steps, underwear of where he was or how he got there not helped by the peak of his head covering his eyes, as well as not knowing what he had done with his keys.

"David! Where's your key?"

"Wouldn't you like to know?" David answered as he shrugged his broad shoulders and hands in the air. Henry turned to Ernest who was having problems with Thomas.

"Do you know where he keeps his door key?"

"Try his trouser pockets the one which had Ernests' friendship card. Everything goes in there, and I mean everything."

Ernest wanted as he twitched his nose slightly as if he was going to sneeze.

"Fuck. OK."

Fondling around inside David's pocket, Henry could not help but feel unused and used jollies, ends of a cigarette and a small pocketknife.

"He's touching me. Er… Thomas, he's touching me!" David called out with his hands still in the air.

"Be grateful no one else will," Thomas answered with a roaring laugh. Ernest quickly pulled out his flask from Thomas's pocket and waved it in front of Thomas.

"Got it."

The keys had bits of fluff from the lining of his jean pocket attached to them.

"Come on."

Pushing David away down the passage, Henry walked behind him. David dripped and fell up on the concrete steps to the main entrance door of the block of flats.

Walking sideways, Henry put the key into the lock and as quietly as possible opened the door and pushed David in.

"Night."

Pulling the door shut, he put the keys through the letter flap just and turned to walk down the steps, and a mighty crash came from inside.

"Fucking bastard!"

David had either fallen or tripped over something that made Henry a smile.

"Right, come on."

Henry placed Thomas's arm around his neck to help Ernest with Thomas's weight. A voice came from across the road.

The pair stopped.

He turned to see the man in the grey suit standing across the road hovering in the alleyway.

"You know him then?" Ernest spoke in a harsh tone.

"Yeah, look… um… wait here I won't be long."

Dropping Thomas, made Ernest stumble backwards.

"Wait, Henry! You."

Puffing his cheeks out, he continued to go off around the corner and disappeared. Henry watched him for a moment as a heavy, deep gut feeling of your pain and sickness filled him as he got closer to the man that obviously believe that he could use any boy he wanted including Henry.

The man flat was a basic plan. No pictures as such only once's of naked young boys and items filled with nothing but sexual acts. The bed draped in white and pink bed duvet and pillow said. It was where he was often sent to as a young fourteen-year-old rent boy. Getting closer, Henry's heart began to pound hard and fast as the man sank into the darkness. Only his green eyes showed like a cat.

"What do you want?"

The man walked in front of Henry forcing his back to the wall.

"You never lost your blond hair." He touched Henry's hair making him freeze at the spot. "Have a look at my cock for me. Would you?" Unzipping his trouser, Henry never moved his eyes just staring at the man deep into his eyes.

"Go on."

"Fuck you."

"You!" Rejection was not an option. It only fuelled him that at times aroused him, as his fingers wrapped around Henry's throat and pushed him hard against the wall.

"You forget who you are? And what you are? Now let's have a look at you."

The man's other hand pulled out Henry's trouser button, with a crude cold stare upon his face.

"Fuck this," Henry said as he found the strength to raise his leg and quickly forced it up in between the man's legs causing the man's mouth to open wide and an agonising cry releasing Henry's throat and falling down on his knees.

Henry first curled up to where his knuckles went white. He raised it up in the air, and with such brute force, he crushed the man's face.

His face threw site on his long black hair that flew across his pale face. Not able to control himself, Henry smashed his face making some sort of deep breathing as his fist repeated the hits until blood came from the man's mouth.

The red curtain went up causing him to stop.

"If you ever, ever touch me like that again, I'll fucking kill you!" Kicking him in the stomach, he made him gargle.

"Get up, you dirty bastard."

Crawling like a dog, he brushed his hair away from his face to show the damage Henry had caused.

"That's OK. You will pay for this." The wall was now his support as he made his way down the alleyway and back into the darkness as Henry watched for a moment.

It was not safe to turn his back. He walked backwards as he got to the safe place in the streets. Henry walked back to Witton Road and back to Ernest.

"Here we go, Thomas. Home sweet home."

Finding the spare key under the mat, Ernest opened the door pushing Thomas inside, following not far behind. Trying not to wake Bella, he carefully led Thomas into the living room. Bella used to keep the house clean like a hospital floor where one could eat their food off the floor. Smells of polish bleach and disinfectant were always present.

"Take your bloody cap and coat off for fuck's sake."

Throwing them onto the old worn and torn armchair, Ernest could feel the cold coming through the window. The heaters had been off a while as Thomas flopped himself down on the two-seater chair falling asleep. It was a thin tartan blanket that covers Thomas up. Bella appeared in the doorway.

"Thank you for bringing him home. If he had to get himself here, God knows where he may have ended up: the cop shop or a whore's bed."

"Not a problem; he's a mate, so it's only right to look after him."

She could never tell whether Ernest was happy or sad as he always had a sullen look on his pale face.

"Where's David?"

"Gone home."

"And Henry?"

Ernest just shrugged his shoulders as he told her that some bloke in a grey suit wanted to speak to him.

Since their friendship turned to much more four years ago, Henry had become overly protective of Ernest to the point of obsession.

"Look, I... um... better go. Got work in the morning."

"Fine. Well. Thanks again."

Ernest gave a smile of sorts as he walked past her, tapping her arm.

"I'll see you out."

"Na, I know the way out."

"Bye, Ernest."

"Night."

Hearing the door shut too Bella just looked on at Thomas as he snored making the edge of his moustache blow just above his top lip.

Hands in his coat pocket and collar up, Ernest made his short walk home.

There were no lights. He opened the flat door, chucked his keys on the small table and switched on the light only to find Henry sitting on the sofa.

"Henry?"

No reply.

"Henry? You alright? What's happened?" Walking across the room looking down at him, he saw Henry's hand red and sore.

Knelt down in front of him, Ernest could see that Henry was crying.

"It was him from that fucking club."

"The gentlemen's club you mean?" Ernest answered nervously as he wrapped his arms around Henry's waist and Henry held Ernest tight with his eyes closed.

"Will you take me to bed?"

"I will... I will, Henry."

Getting up on his feet, Ernest took Henry's hand and led him to the bedroom.

Their lovemaking was always tender, slow and careful enough that he did not hurt Ernest. As they laid down naked, Henry gently crested Ernest's body with no more than kisses about his neck, lips and slowly down his whole body towards his hip, then between his legs, which caused him to open his mouth and take deep breaths.

"Oh... oh... Hen... Henry... mmm..."

A sensation ran through his thin body as he felt him kiss and suckle at him till, he felt himself swell and come. As Henry made his way back towards Ernest's face, he took Ernest's hand and placed it between his legs. Henry never had anything like this between his legs other than Ernest who knew how to make him swell and come slowly.

"Please. I want you inside me."

Rolling him over Henry guided Ernest as he always did inside of him.

It was always with tender loving care and warmth as Ernest placed his hand on Henry's back gently so as not to hurt the deep cuts that covered his back.

"Oh, God."

"I... I'm not hurting you oh."

"Oh, please. No."

Holding himself, Henry and Ernest began to swell until they finally become wet. Ernest pushed once more, and Henry told him not to move from him and stay there.

A moment passed, Ernest finally climbed off him and laid down.

Henry pulled his lover into him as he fell asleep in Henry's arms.

"I love you, Henry."

Kissing Ernest's thick black hair, Henry tightened his hold.

"And I love you. Don't ever leave me."

"I won't. I want you to stay with me always."

The darkness outside was blacker as the grey moon showed very little on the empty streets below. Silence everywhere. No one was there outside but the sound of the rain tapping upon the windows and the cold air causing the droplets to look as though the rain could walk, and yet at that moment, nothing could come between them.

No one would dare.

Chapter 2
Threats and Ideas

The jewellery quarter was no more than a fifteen-minute walk from the city centre. It was small yet filled with expensive items.

Ideas filled David's mind with how to make money and what better than to have it protected and yet not really his style.

The small cafe in the city had become a place for the Brummie boys of Aston to meet up in the morning or at least until the pubs opened.

The place was filled with smoke thick in the air, and tables were not yet cleared.

David had ordered his cup of coffee and waited for Thomas to arrive.

The morning air was fresh, and a cold breeze came up the street as Thomas made his way into the cafe.

As he walked in, an urge to look around at the tables to check for people who may want to cause him trouble or the police. Looking towards the back of the café, He saw David sat there head down just the top of his snapback cap with the word cat at the front in bright yellow. Thomas never understood his young friend's fashion.

Henry was in ripped dark blue jeans, a black T-shirt and a biker jacket.

Ernest was in the ripped jeans only in black a white T-shirt and a chunky blue cardigan, but at least they looked smart apart from their black combat boots. David just looked like a damp.

As he said down, Thomas wrapped his long brown coat around him as his jumper did not keep all the cold out.

"So? What was it that you needed to talk to me about? It's better be good as my fucking head is banging and my mouth is as dry as the Sahara Desert."

David leant in across his steaming cup of coffee. His voice was croaky and his breath smelt bad.

"There's a small shop just down the way from here, and there is an old man, Jewish, I think."

"So?"

"So... He is having problems with small time crooks, a man who think they are intimidating but not really."

Thomas rubbed his forehead staring down at the table.

"I really don't know what this has got to do with us?"

David grew a mad hatters' grin across his unclean face and told him about how much the old man is finding it hard to protect his business and not willing to go to the police for fear of having his windows smashed in.

"Well, it's a better idea than that other stupid one of the racecourses. No one does that anymore."

Crossing his legs, Thomas leaned back into his chair and took out his packet of cigarettes and a small box of swan matches.

"As if I didn't know better. Who...? Are you planning to send for this new venture of yours?"

"Henry."

"That's what I was afraid of. Look, you do know that he's on a knife's edge already, and what makes you seriously think he will do it?"

It was Ernest who entered, walked and towards his friend's table.

"What…?"

It had become harder to separate Ernest from Henry these days as they spent very little time with others.

Ernest decided to stand on the corner of Witton Road near the pharmacy waiting for Henry, but as he had slept, then he would go on his own.

The bedroom had gone cold as Henry woke from his sleep only to find Ernest had gone. But a note was on his pillow.

> Just waiting here at the pharmacy
> at the corner of Witton Road. See you there.
> Love you,
> Ernest Xxx

Henry finished dressing straightening his jacket collar. He felt something in his jacket pocket as he took out his hand a bunch of rolled-up notes of about a thousand pound easy if not more were trapped up by an elastic band.

Henry remembered taking it from the man's pocket as he laid face down after Henry brutally attacked him.

Pushing the money back into his inside code pocket with a smile on his face, he left the flat locking it up and making his way out the block of flats and out into the cold streets.

"Ernest?"

"Thank God. You took your fucking time!"

Henry just gave the sweetest smile as he walked close, very close to him and took Ernest's arm.

"What you doin' standin' on the corner like a whore?"

"The jewellery shop."

"Oh, crap. Now?"

"Yeah, come on."

The pair never said much to each other yet knew what the other was thinking.

It is a tiny, old-fashioned small, whatever you would like to call it. The old man had worked hard for it, and the group of only three men came to demand money. This had become a scene that he had become accustomed to.

"Come on, old man. Just cough up whatever you have, and we'll leave you alone."

The old man feared for his life begging them to leave his shop alone, which only caused them to give cackle laugh showing their rotten teeth and the smell of something that was not drunk or normal cigarettes.

As they moved their way towards the back of the counter, the doorbell rang as someone came in.

"Mornin'!"

Henry spoke out loud enough to make his and Ernest's presence known.

Ernest bolted the door, turned the 'Closed' sign around and pull down the blind as Henry strolled up to the glass counter and casually leaned against it.

The brute that now had the old man cowering for his life left him for a moment while looking at Henry in a way of the wanting to cause some sort of injury, but Henry just turned to look down at the glass counter as though he was browsing through the jewellery.

"Fuck me. The two of the Brummie boys of Aston." The brute was now so close to Henry as he could feel the brute breathe upon the side of his face.

"You've heard of us then?"

It was as though Henry was trying to show him up in front of those around him fuelled by anger. He turned to his followers nodding towards them to corner Ernest.

"People like yourself should really get over the whole skinhead thing. It's all over." Henry turned his head to face the brute with a strained face.

"Oh, yes? And you'd know all about skinheads."

"Yeah, I do actually."

The brute gave a smile showing barely any teeth in his mouth.

"That's right. You were a rent boy for." The brute the said and panted like a dog in Henry's face. It did not seem to be bothered by the reaction. He wanted, but looking at his followers and nodding his head, he turned back to Henry.

One of them went for Ernest, but as he did so, Ernest took out a small piece of iron pipe and smash the man's side with it taking his sight off the other who grabbed Ernest by the throat and forced him up against to door causing in Henry's blood to boil as he heard Ernest back cracking against the door.

Quick and violently, Henry pushed the brute headfirst on to the glass counter leaning his whole upper body on him pushing his face into the glass that the old man believed his head may go through it.

Pulling the brute's arm up his back as far as he could, he forced it to the point of breaking it.

"You get your bastards of my friend right now otherwise I will split the vein in your rest and leave you to fuckin' bleed to death in the gutter. Alright!"

"OK, OK. For Christ's sake, let the little bastard go. Please!" The brute sounded as though he was about to cry.

Releasing Ernest's throat, the brute was pulled back up and thrown across the floor. Despite Henry's five feet, it only took someone to even touch Ernest to become stronger.

"Get the fuck out and came back here again. I will swear to God I'll kill ya!"

Ernest moved out the way coughing and holding his throat as he unbolted the door to unlock it and then out into the street stumbling.

Henry went up to Ernest to check that he was not marked.

"You alright?"

"Yeah, yeah, I'm fine. Thank you."

The pair just stared into each other's eyes but were broken by the old man's voice.

"Please no violence. Please."

"We're here to help you," Ernest answered as he looked past Henry who turned round to face in the same direction.

"We're here to give you protection against people like that."

"Please I do not need protection. The police…," Henry and Ernest giggled.

"The cops? You've just had someone come in threatening your life and shop, and there was no cop around. Don't be funny. You can't control it. So we're here to offer you help."

The place went silent for a moment.

"Please."

"Look, I'll make it easy for you. You give me your float from the till, and we'll go."

"I have no money in the till."

"Liar." Ernest reacted quickly as he found his voice. Henry was losing his patience. He could think of better things he could do with his time, most of it spend with Ernest.

"Look, I am tired, and I've got to get to work. So!"

Henry stood at the door. His hand held out.

"For now, we'll leave you alone."

"Henry!"

"Shhh, and don't tell no one what you saw understand."

The old man nodded as he took the palm of his hand where his heart was. Opening the till, the old man handed the thirty-pound float.

"Good, oh, and if you have any other problem, meet us at the pub. Enjoy your day."

Pushing Ernest out the door and turning the 'Closed' sign back around, the pair left and made their way into town.

The walk was slow and silent, and with only the sound of cars driving by, Henry stopped for a moment.

"What is it?" Weary of asking, Ernest stopped behind him.

"Come on." Henry nodded to a back street alley where it was lonely and quiet, and nobody was around. Ernest took it as a sign for a long kiss much to Henry's delight.

Their kisses were always slow and gentle as he held Ernest's face until he was finished.

"That's better."

Henry gave a small cough and smile.

"That's not what I was going to ask for, but it was a lovely surprise. Do it again."

Never able to say no to the man he loved. The two young men were embraced lovingly with hands flowing over each other until Henry pulled out the roll of notes in front of Ernest causing him to stop.

"Where did you get that from?"

Ernest let Henry go and took the money from him. Looking at it, it was a roll of notes wrapped in an elastic band.

"The bastard who tried it on with me? Remember?"

"Yeah?"

"After I beaten him, I must have taken it from his pocket."

Ernest went into a moment of shock.

"You stole it."

"No, no, my love. I took it for us. Only for us."

Henry spoke softly as he held Ernest by his hips.

"Well? What do you want all this for?"

"Our future."

Ernest popped it back into Henrys' jacket pocket before embracing Henry again.

It was in a small room upstairs above a closed town shop that Thomas had happily rented from an old army mate ideal for a new scheme.

"Well? What do you think?" Thomas asked proudly as he showed David around a room despite its derelict empty shell David seemed quite happy with it.

"At least no one will know about it. No one downstairs. No neighbours. That sort of thing now about my last venture."

Thomas sat down on a stool leaning against the cold brick wall crossing his legs and placing his raw flesh hands upon his knee.

"And may I dare ask what this new venture is?" David sat himself on the floor, gritty under foot and wiped his hands on his jeans taking his head off.

"Bookmaking."

Thomas moved his head very so slightly backwards. His eyes focused on David.

"Bookmaking? As in illegal betting?"

"Yeah, why not? I mean that. Let's face it. No one really know. Wants people to know how much they bet. Here it would be private. No one needs to know, and we are making a living."

"Three of us already do."

David gave a sudden abrupt laughter leaning backwards.

"That's what you call it? You earn fuck. At least, with this, we pay out, and David drew a circle with his forefinger. 'We also get paid'."

Thomas got up and went over to the broken window to look out for a moment.

"OK, alright, just say. And I mean just say we go through with this? How are we meant to get punters? From where?" Thomas asked in a deep smokey voice shrugging his shoulders.

A sick look came across David's face. His eyes went black that told Thomas that he already knew who he was going to use.

"No, don't. Don't use him."

"Why not? He's quite never been in trouble with the law, and he's the sort to go about his business without getting caught."

Thomas took a deep breath and rubbed his face with his hands.

"If you use Ernest? Henry will kill you. You know what he's like not just that, but young Ernest is only five foot nothing if he gets into trouble. We won't be there to help."

"All the more reason to use him lesser. You and I are a bit taller and older than him with a history of criminal offences; it makes sense to use him."

"No, I don't like it. Sorry, but no… no chance. Think of another Idea. Anything but not that."

David turned his head to look at the far wall and went quiet making Thomas feel uncomfortable.

The pub was filled to the point of bursting smoke from pipes and cigarettes filled the atmosphere, drinks being spilt with the sound of glasses being broken along with roars of laughter.

Ernest pushed his way through the crowd trying to collect the empties while Henry served the drinks along with George, and who he could sing along, Ernest got behind the bar.

A local band had been paid to play any modern music to the drinker's courts along with causing Henry and Ernest to dance at times behind the bar.

"ER… OI! KID! PUT ANOTHER IN THERE!" shouted a punter handing his empty to Ernest. The bar was small and tight leaving very little room to move. George told the lads to stay behind the bar while he collected the empties. It was easier as George was a fair size.

At times, with a bar overwhelmed, Henry and Ernest were close to each other. Henry placed his hands on Ernest's hips to move him, which naturally Ernest never minded.

Bull's-eye was one of those men that believed he owned Aston. He was a short pig-faced bald man, well-known for using women and rent boys for money, but on this night, he was noticed as he walked in an air of arrogance about him as he walked through the door.

"O! No fucking fighting alright. Otherwise, you're barred."

"You can't bar me from what I own!"

"You don't know shit! This is my pub, I own it. Move!" but it never seemed to bother Bull's-eye who disfigured his face walking over to the bar where Ernest and Henry stood near the back where the bottles and glasses were placed.

"Boy!"

Ernest looked at him and then back to Henry, who went to serve him.

"NOT YOU... HENRY!" Pointing his fat stumpy finger at Ernest willing to go over, gently push Henry back on the stool.

"What do you want? Usual?"

"Please."

Taking the pint glass from a shelf under the bar and to the pump, Ernest tipped it. As he poured it, Bull's-eye watched with a crushed-up face.

"I hear you're fucking around." Bull's eye spoke in a hoarsy voice as he leaned over the bar.

"No. I haven't been fucking around," Ernest answered silently.

"Of course, you haven't. That's not what I have heard."

"Like I said. I don't fuck around. And, if I do bed a man, it's only one," Ernest answered as he slammed the filled pint glass down and put his hand out for the money. Holding the money out, Ernest went to snatch it, but Bull's-eye grabbed him by the wrist gripping and squeezing as a python would do to its prey.

Bull's-eye forced his fat stomach against the bar so that his face was up in Ernest's.

"I know all about you."

"Get off him, Bull's-eye!" George gave his first warning as he came up from behind him.

George was not a man to be messed with especially on a Saturday night. As Thomas had shown up, Bull's-eye's threw Ernest's wrist from his grip. Ernest moved rubbing his wrist.

Pushing and shoving people around, Thomas went to the far side of the bar. Henry followed him to serve him.

"Whiskey... after what I've just between told make it double."

Henry looked over his shoulder at his friends in a concerned way.

"Go on. What is it?"

The glass hit the wooden bar.

"Come here."

Leaning over the bar, arms crossed Henry listened to Thomas telling him about the empty shop in town and David's new venture into illegal gambling as well as who he was planning to use as a runner pointing over towards Ernest's direction. Henry turned to look at Ernest and then back to Thomas who had knocked back the double and pushed the glass towards his young friend whose friendly face had changed.

"Over my fuckin' dead body, trying to use my Ernest," shrugging his shoulders and pulling his old worn black peak cap, Henry grabbed the glass and went back to refill it as Ernest went towards the back of the bar and lent on the till.

"Thomas, OK?"

"Don't ask. You don't want to know."

"HENRY!" bellowed out a voice from the front of the bar.

Henry knew who it was but made him wait as he gave Thomas another double before going over to Bull's-eye.

"I want a word with you."

As though he did not care, Henry strolled over to him and leaned his elbow on the edge of the bar.

"You owe me."

"For what?" Henry replied pulling a face making an expansion upon his face, and shrugging his shoulders, he could not help but notice Bull's-eye's foul breath and rotten teeth. He never changed.

"You owe me a fuck."

"No, I don't."

"If you don't do what I ask big, I'll go for Ernest."

Filled with big anger and boiling blood, Henry leaned over so he was face-to-face with Bull's-eye.

"You do not fucking own me anymore. And don't you ever threaten me either."

"Why? Can't he force himself?" Bull's-eye never got the chance to finish his sentence as Henry threw himself over the bar pushing Bull's-eye into the crowd and taking out a table. Henry used his fist as he repeatedly hit Bull's-eye across the face while holding his throat as if he was going to choke him to death making a crowd from shouting out for him to finish Bull's-eye off, but as it got out of hand, George pushed his way through and grabbed Henry from under his armpits and dragged him off.

"PACK IT IN THE PAIR OF YA! HENRY LEAVE IT! LEAVE IT!"

Held back by two blokes as he watched the man who destroyed his teenage years roll and get up like a slug up off the floor only helped by a wooden stool!

"OUT! YOU GET OUT!" George ordered as he pointed at the big wooden doors.

Embarrassed by what had happened, Bull's-eye pushed his way through the roaring crowd who poked at him as he fell out the door and into the streets. Walking towards the entrance that led behind the bar. George stopped him.

"YOU alright, babs?"

"Yeah, yeah. I'm fine." Turning his head towards Ernest who stood near a drunken Thomas, he looked back at the crowd.

"WHO'S NEXT?" Revving the crowd up, Henry went back behind the bar and carried on as if nothing had happened.

"You coming?" Thomas asked as he waited for his friends. The pub had gone quiet as closing time finally arrived.

"Where?" Henry had forgotten about the venture as he and Ernest started cleaning up.

"Take a fucking wild guess?"

"We can't. We have to clean up," Ernest answered as he popped up from behind the bar with a concerned expression on his face.

"Na, it's okay. You two go on. I'll clear up, but the broken table can wait when you come in tomorrow morning to clean the lines. Henry I'm looking at you."

"Fair enough." Henry didn't argue as Ernest handed him his jacket and headed towards the door.

"Night, George!"

"Yeah, yeah."

Walking into town, Thomas and Henry walked side by side while Ernest just strolled behind them.

"Dare I ask, but what was all that about? With Bull's-eye I mean?" Thomas asked with caution as he handed Henry a cigarette.

"Nothing important."

"No. Cause not." Thomas could not help but let out a giggle as Henry lit up his fag.

"Come on, lad! I need to get home tonight!" Thomas shouted out to a tired Ernest.

"Why?"

"Never you mind."

The alleyway was dark and narrow as they made their way to the iron staircase. As they made their way up, the cool air cut through them.

BANG! BANG! BANG!

Thomas could not bang the door any harder with his fist and shouting out David to open up with the sounds of bolts and key unlocking the door as they pushed their way in only for Henry and Ernest to go into shock at the state of the room.

"Done up on the cheap, it would look half decent," Henry said to himself.

"Well? Fucking say something?"

David was on a high full of excitement as he stood there legs apart and arms open wide with a smile upon his dirty face.

"It's… Um…," Ernest answered as he just looked out the windows that had been smashed in some time and a door that they just came through was nearly off its hinges, and the cold was soaked in with dampness that you could smell.

Henry went walking over to the windows that looked out over the other side of the building as he watched four young lads walking with a badly bruised Bull's-eye, no doubt another house where they would be rented out. All he could was pray that they knew what would happen to them just as Thomas looked across the room and noticed Henry looking outside and went over to him.

"Henry?"

"Yeah?"

"You OK, babs?"

"Yeah, I'm fine. Just watching four young bastards with Bull's-eye."

"Bastards. Sick bastards."

"Well? I got lucky."

Thomas smiled as he put his hand on Henry's shoulder as Henry turned to look at Ernest who was talking away to David who popped a small red book and pencil into Ernest's cardigan pocket.

"You now know what you have to do, right?"

"I guess, but why me?"

"Coz... just... coz." David could not answer him so he patted his friend on the arm.

"See, Thomas! I told you he'd do it."

Thomas signalled as if he was cutting his own throat as a warning to shut it, then pointing at Henry who looked back at Thomas.

"What's he talking about?"

"Well... now... see..."

Anger once more showed in Henry's eyes as he turned and walked up to David and Ernest and stood between them.

Looking at Ernest straight into his brown eyes (that he had always loved). Ernest was too scared to answer as he knew. Henry could change very quickly.

"He'll be fine." David's voice made Henry shrive as he turned to face him.

"Why? Do you want to go?" David asked as Henry's brain said to him. Never waiting to scare Ernest, he started to walk off.

"Aww! What's the matter, Henry? Don't worry. He'll be home in time to suck you off!"

Upon hearing that, Thomas felt like putting his head into a deep hole as Ernest was close to the spot hearing David laughing. He turned his back on Henry.

It was too quick when Henry was back and headed to David while removing his belt and warping it around his wrist. The belt buckle was thick and heavy. On occasions, Ernest had seen Henry use it on other fellas who had tried it on or touched Ernest. It was always horrific.

David could see Henry through the broken glass and fearing him he garbed a metal pole, which laid on the floor, picked it up and swung it.

"COME ON THEN, YOU FUCKING POOF!"

Swinging it on, Henry went towards him making Ernest and Thomas back up against the far wall.

The fight was violent.

Henry dodged as the pole swung at him causing him to hit the floor. David stood over him, raised to pole and brought it down, and Henry managed to roll away as it came down clanging hard on the floor.

Thomas could see someone getting killed. It was most likely David.

Screaming out in fear, Thomas very stupidly got between the two fired-up young men. Out of breath and hot, they pulled themselves apart, but as usual, David got to a stop, threw the pole down and turned his back, but as he walked away, he could not help himself and made a remain about Ernest and Henry.

Henry finally lost it and walked up on him. Wrapping the belt around David's neck and bucked it up quick enough so he could pull it up and choke David.

Riddling and unable to talk, David fought to breathe "WO!"

Ernest sprinted as quickly as he could to stop Henry from throttling David.

"Let him go. Henry, please for me," Ernest begged as he pulled Henry who finally let go leaving the belt still strapped around David's threat. Thomas ran over to help David who was lying flat on the floor. Thomas pulled on the buckle and tried to get it off as David started to change colour.

"Don't pull it," David spoke in a mouse-like voice lifting David to sit upright Thomas finally unbuckled the belt as David dropped to the floor holding his throat and gasping for air. Thomas handed Ernest the belt as he helped David up onto his feet.

"What did I tell ya! Hay? What did you say?"

Demanding an answer, Thomas smacked David who was coughing but watching Henry from the corner of his eye as Thomas hit him once more across his head.

Embarrassed and felt shown up by what had just happened, David never answered his older friend and headed towards the door.

"Ernest?" David tried to shout out, but his voice sounded crooked and sore.

"What now?" Ernest spoke softly as he still held Henry back by placing his hand on Henry's chest, he could feel his love's heart pounding hard.

"Tomorrow morning! Don't forget!"

"No, I won't forget. I'll do it."

David gave a death look at Henry who moved very close to Ernest as he put his belt back onto his jeans.

"Out! Everyone out," Thomas ordered them outside as they went towards the door.

As they made their way down the iron staircase, he stopped to lock up so no one knew that anyone had been there.

The walk back to their homes was silent as David walked on ahead rubbing his throat and his head filled with ideas of how to get at Henry and leave him gasping for air.

Chapter 3
Witton Road

"Morning," Bella spoke softly as she sat at the kitchen table with a cup of coffee warming her rough hands.

"Morning," Thomas was often quiet first thing in the morning more often so when he had been drinking heavily.

"Where you off to?"

"Work."

Bella fell silent for a moment as she looked into her cup as Thomas helped himself to a cup of tea. "Where were you last night? You are very late last night. Later than normal. And that's never a good thing, especially if it involves the others."

Thomas had barely finished his cup as Bella threw every question at him as fast as she could. "What do you want me to say? Hay! I went to the pub, so Henry and Ernest, and came home."

"I just want to know because I care."

"Well, don't fucking care. I'm not worth caring about."

"Thomas!"

Storming down the hallway, Thomas put on his cap and carried his brown coat out the door just as Bella got closer.

"Thomas! Please! I'm sorry."

The neighbours were as nosy even more so since Bella showed up some five years earlier.

"What are you lot fucking starring at! Thomas…"

"I'm off to work."

Looking across the street, she stuck her middle finger up in the air, leaving to go back inside slamming the front door hard.

The butchers had taken Thomas on after the Falklands War. He had come home a very different man and never spoke of what happened only to Henry who had fought a very different war. Norman was a very kind man always willing to help anyone no matter who it was seeing Thomas wondering the streets just as he had come out of the hospital.

Norman decided to take him on and give him a room until he had sorted himself out. It was until one morning while he was at the back hung over. Thomas was cutting meat up with a sharp meat cleaver that without warning Norman who was out front heard the worst kind of scream come from out back.

Panic set in when he went out to only see Thomas holding his hand blood dripping from his hand onto the worktops and down to the floor with three fingers on the chopping board recognizable for losing his fingers on the left hand.

"Morning, boss."

"Good morning, young man. How are you?"

"Well, considering I went out last night at the pub, sober, really. Why?"

"News has got around the fight that broke out."

Not replying Thomas removed his cap and coat rolled up his sleeves and donned his red and white striped apron on and made his way to the counter.

"Good morning, Mrs Wilson. And what can I get you this morning?"

A bit worried but not willing to push for an answer Norman went out the back to pop the kettle on.

Mrs Wilson was a lady in her eighties and well-known to Thomas. A lovely lady who always remembered to give out Christmas and Easter cards to everyone right down to the street cleaner.

As well as a Christian woman she cared about people her help when Thomas was made homeless due to his drinking habits made her a special person in his eyes and that was rare as only Bella had a special place in his heart.

"I'll have half a pound of liver pigs please."

"Of course."

"Oh and some smoky bacon as well. Please…"

Thomas weighed it all and began to bag it up for her.

"Keeping warm my handsome?"

"As warm as you can be Mrs Wilson."

Looking to check that no one was around she lent in as close as she could across the meat counter.

"Err…"

Thomas lent in to hear her better.

"I'd like to place a bet I've heard about your taking 'em."

"Oh now MRS Wilson…"

"No, no. Now I'll let you decide on what horse you see, my neighbour her husband well he told her about what is happening and well here."

Pushing five pounds into Thomas's hand she gave a sweet smile as if butter wouldn't melt not knowing that Norman was watching carefully and with suspicion.

"Everything alright out here, Tom!"

"Yeah, yeah! Just having a chin wag with Mrs Wilson."

Mrs Wilson just gave a quick wink and finally left with her to meet for the week.

"Who's next? Yes, madam, what can I get you?"

Thomas covered up too quickly for Norman to grasp what was going on.

Bella very rarely if ever went to the shops these days fear of the streets brought back her days spent 'working' them, but this time she had no choice as they were running low on milk.

The rain had made the streets feel colder than usual will people walking around minding their own business but there were those who remember her very well, especially the men who most likely explained why Endicott Road was a relief.

"Good morning, Mr Pyke."

"Morning, our wench. How are you this morning?"

Bella was waived in by the lonely old lady as for just over a year ago Bella had taken in washing for Mrs Pyke who was a widow and her only child Peter had winkled in the Falklands War, yet she would be seen popping out first thing in the morning and again just as dusk fell looking down the road in hope that he would come home.

He never will.

Walking through the living room into the kitchen, Mrs Pyke pulled out a small back of washing and handed it to Bella.

"There is also something I have for you."

Going over to the friendship old out some left our beef wrapped in Grease prove paper.

"Here, babs. For you thought, you could make something out of it for yourself and them boys."

Bella's mouth opened a jar and saw the roast beef just enough for four. What a treat.

"Mrs Pyke, I can't."

"Now here." Handing her a little container with dripping inside.

Bella felt the warm tears form in her beautiful brown eyes as they trickled down her cheeks.

"You've always been so very kind, but I don't deserve it. Not after what I have done."

"Now you just listen to me, my girl. If my Peter was here he'd of married you and I know that for a fact and as he is not here yet it is my job to look after you until he does come home."

"Thank you," wiping her cheeks with the back of her hand there were movements of silence between the two women as Peter's photo in his army uniform took the pride of place in the living room, bedroom even the kitchen.

"Now come on drive your eyes and on your way."

"I'll get this back to you by tomorrow afternoon."

"No rush. You look after yourself and get home safe."

Walking Bella out, she watched her walk down the path waving her off and quickly checking to see if Peter was about before finally going indoors.

Bella knew Peter. They were good friends before the war broke out and often spoke about one day getting married.

The day he left she made him promise that if he came home safe he would marry him. Peter wanted that more than anything else in the world but after he had been killed a small Ring with Bella's photo was found amongst his things the ring was given to her as she now wore it around her neck on a fine necklace chain yet his death hit her hard and she found herself on the streets as a prostitute for Bull's-eye.

It was not until Thomas took her in, but in return, she has to take care of his house: cook, clean and iron his cloth, and have sex with him when he wanted it.

Complete opposite of Peter.

Walking through the front door she could see Thomas was sitting at the kitchen table looking into his empty tea cup.

As he sat there with a cigarette lit, he wasted no time to ask her where she'd been.

Fear struck her as Thomas smashed the little bag from her and tipped it upside down causing the beef and the container with the dripping rolled on to the table.

"I was at Mrs Pykes. I am doing some washing for her and…"

There was no point continuing her conversation as she watched him, rip the beef apart like a wild animal, Ernest who was stood next to the sink, just watched in shock. In Ernest eyes it was one thing to fight men but treat those you say you love how could you treat them this way. Ernest just smiled and gently touched her arm.

"Let me take that washing for you. You go and sit down. I'll pop the kettle on for you."

"Get me one!" Thomas demanded as he filled his face.

Bella just turned and whispered to herself …

"Get it your fucking self."

Chapter 4
Debbie

David had lately seemed to become distracted. He had become obsessed with a more secret way of making money.

"Go on then. What is it?"

Henry couldn't help but ask as he and David, much to everyone shock given their dislike for each other, walked down the street. One of many as they have been in every single pub in Aston drinking no more than one drink in each pub causing Henry to become fed up as he was the one buying the drinks.

The bookmaking helped him make money but not as fast as David wanted.

"OI! What is it?"

"Mmm…" said David.

"Fuck it never mind."

The doors to the pub swung open and two well-built men off their heads on drinks fell out into the streets as Henry and David just stood there and watched them fall.

"Come on."

David gave a quick tug on his friends' quote as he started to walk inside.

"I work here. Why would I want to drink here?"

Henry called out in a foul mood, tired and fed up, and money was now running low in his pockets as he put his hands into his jacket pocket. David reached out and grabbed him by his collar and pulled him in.

The pub was packed to the brim as usual at this time of the evening. Men were laughing their heads off in drink; smoke was thick and heavy; women were sitting near the windows with pints.

David's eyes began to wander around the room scanning it like a machine gun.

"What or who were you looking for? I'm getting fed up with moving round the town. And I'm cold and hungry."

"Oh shut it. Come on; we'll sit over there near the bogs."

Forcing David through the crowd towards the back of the pub near the toilets, the smell was overwhelming causing Henry's guts to roll.

"Fucking hell."

"Just sit the fuck down. Get me a pint before you sit your ass down. Thank you."

Henry looked up sharply as he was just about the pull his chair out from under the table. Frustrated by David's weird attitude, he did not argue and left him to go up to the bar.

Sitting back in a chair and looking around the crowded room, David looked on the edge of his nerves.

"Come on, you stupid bitch. Where the fuck are ya?"

Talking to himself as he intertwined his fingers and laid his hands on his stomach.

The bar was crammed as punters crowded around it or leaning on it for support after having too many. Henry pushed his way through the bar and ordered his small whiskey and David's pint. He found himself scanning the room when he noticed that he got the eye of two young lads: one small stature with ginger curly hair and pale complexion and the other fair hair and pale.

Henry gave a little solute, then turned back to the barman. He could see them giggling like little girls.

"Not a fuckin' chance," he said under his breath as he made his way back to the table where the crowds were now gathering, but David refused to leave.

"Whoever we are waiting for better show up soon, I'm fucking off home. I hate being away from..."

"Ernest? Don't worry; you'll have plenty of time to fuck him."

Henry glared at him as he slammed the full pint glass down and sat himself down pulling from his coat pocket a packet of cigarettes.

Rolling one up and cupping it in between his thin lips, he lit up and blew the smoke out from his mouth.

"She'll turn up."

"She better."

Frustrated and anxious David stood up on his chair as Henry looked on.

"What the fuck are you doing now? Sit down just sit the fuck down, DAVID."

"Here, she's here!"

"Oh, thank god for that. Can I go now?"

"No!"

Rolling his eyes and pulling his collar up, Henry sat back in his chair and continue to drag on his cigarette.

"Sorry, I'm late for work. It was work. The bitch kept us on longer."

The woman spoke in a husky voice. She was only forty, and yet she looked older.

David climbed down and held her upper arm.

"Henry, this is."

"Debbie. Yeah, I know her."

"Hello Henry."

David looked on confused until she told him that Henry and she worked for Bull's-eye unable to hear his sick past being dragged up again, Henry necked his drink back, smiled and left as he noticed the two young lads started to follow him.

"So have you got it?" Debbie asked anxiously and bent her knees as though she needed the toilet.

"I do here."

Pulling out of his trouser pocket was a small brown paper bag, but it was what she was gagging for.

Crack cocaine.

Stretching now to grab the bag, her veins showed in her hands. Her wrist was grabbed and forced down to her side.

"There is a price to pay," David softly spoke with his glittering eyes.

"I don't have any money."

"Well now, isn't that a shame?"

"But I may have other things I think you may want to have."

Grabbing his coat and taking Debbie's hand, the pair pushed their way through the crowd for the door. Laughing, they made their way down an alleyway far in so no more could see them.

Small Heath

The crowd were starting the dwindle as the night slowly came to a close. The landlord had already served Thomas and Ernest four times much to his dislike of them.

They sat towards the door in case they need to get out quickly. It was also away from the smell of the toilets as most of the blokes had gathered around the bar shoving each other. Some were already drunk, and some were halfway there.

"Best to keep our hands down our kid."

"Maybe it wasn't a good idea coming here. I mean coz of who we are."

Thomas leaned towards his young friend. His eyes looked tired, and his face was pale.

"We both agreed to come here because you and I are sick of them; two are fucking going for each other, and I'm sick of the same fucking pub. No disrespect."

"None taken."

The sounds of shattered glass broke their conversation, and they slowly turned their heads towards the bar.

"Looks like someone has been fucking the same woman."

"How can ya tell?"

"Look, the whore that's trying to break them up. I've seen them sort before they stick out a mile."

"You BASTARD!" A small man no more than five feet and greasy hair stood up only face to face to just with the thin six-foot bloke facing him.

"YOU'RE NOT KEEPING HER HAPPY SO SHE CAME TO ME. ALRIGHT!"

Ernest started to feel vulnerable, weak and unguarded at the same time but dare not to show it.

"There he goes." Thomas leaned back into his chair as the thin bloke fell to the ground hard.

"Time to go, Thomas!"

"You might be right, our kid. Come on!"

The tension along with the thick smoke and the smell of beer filled the air.

"Move!"

Thomas went to grab Ernest, but he had disappeared.

"ERNEST! Shit."

"Tom?"

Ernest was now held by two blokes. His stomach exposed as the other man punched him in the stomach.

Ernest felt himself so weak as the man hit a bit too close to his groan. The next blow was straight across his face just catching his eyes.

The final blow hit his ribs causing him to fall to his knees.

Thomas screamed like a madman as he was charged at by another man grasping a glass bottle and a face fuelled with alcohol gridding his teeth. Thomas gave a full-force fist punch causing the man to hit the table behind him.

Ernest fought to keep himself safe as the man came back at him this time hitting and kicking him as Thomas was attacked.

Two thin men hit him full in the face nearly breaking his jaw, nose and ribs. Crawling through the crowd, Thomas grabbed Ernest forcing him to his feet.

"Get up! We've to get the fuck out of here. Come on."

As they approached the door, a man came up from behind them tapping Ernest on the shoulder who finally swung around getting him in the face and causing him to hit the chair that Thomas had sat on, nothing but red mist came before Thomas' face as he kicked the man brutally.

"Don't fucking touch us again, you dirty bastard! Get the fuck off him."

Glasses and stools were now being used as weapons.

"Move your head, our kid!"

Ernest ducked as glass bottles just missed him.

At last, taking hold of Ernest, Thomas got them out into the safety of the streets leaving the brawling crowd behind them.

The air was cold and filled with smoke and fog.

Graffiti covered the brick walls as they struggled to walk in pain.

"We can't take you back to yours. Henry will go absolutely ape shit at me. How am I going to explain this to Bella?"

A guttural sound came as Ernest gradually fell to the ground.

"No, no, no, babes. Come on; let's get you home. God help me."

Pulling his friend to his feet, the pair continued their way home.

The Gully

They were like wild animals.

Their mouths open wide enough that it looked as though they were eating each other allowing the others' tongues to play with the others.

"Oh yes! David, David."

"What, what?"

Debbie whispered as she gripped his jacket collar forcing his face into her neck and guided his hand up under her skirt.

"Go on; fuck me."

David fumbled his trouser zip.

"You're going to love this."

His heart was pounding as she played with him causing him to groan in pleasure.

"Yes, you like that; get inside. It would be a waste otherwise."

Debbie spoke in a deep smoky voice as she placed him inside her.

"OH SHIT YES!"

As they pushed and arched against each other, they felt their hearts and found their heads span. David tilted his head back and looked up into the black sky.

The quicker they went. David looked back at Debbie who now looked like a lunatic, her eyes wild as he had the wall with his fist, they both become wet.

Tired and relieved, David looked at her just looking at her for a moment. He thought that this could be the woman for him yet that thought went as she pushed him away from her and grabbed the paper bag from him.

Debbie gave a sly smile pulling her skirt down. She shoved him out of the way and left leaving a confused man still unable to move.

Henry had stopped to look out for the cut remembering his and Ernest's first night together. Those two young boys made him to think of Ernest.

The bedroom at Ernest's flat was small but cosy. The bed was in the centre of the room; the small bathroom was just off the side. It was a real home even more so to Henry who was just fourteen and away from home as his mother had chosen and abused him for a man.

Finding himself on the streets of Aston, Bull's-eye came in only to use him for money as a rent boy.

His first time was violent and sudden.

Strip to completely naked, the man stood before him forcing him onto the bed as he kissed Henry all over his neck, mouth, face and body down to where he saw his legs spread eagled and very quickly suckled on until he was ruled over onto his stomach and feeling a sharp pain as the man forced himself inside of Henry.

"Dear not to show tears," Henry squeezed his eyes until it was all over. Once the man left, Henry found blood all over his backside. This became a regular thing until the age of eighteen.

Where he stood now was where he got caught by Bull's-eye and two of his men.

"Get him!"

Henry felt one of the men tackle him to the ground hitting his face.

"Get him up; bring him to me!"

Nails pierced his skin as he was wearing only trousers and drainage on. Henry was suddenly pushed once again against the wall facing the river as he watched it run by.

"Run away from me, will you? You little bastard, I'll teach your lesson you won't forget," Bull's-eye whispered in Henry's ear as he turned him to face the wall and braced himself. He felt Bull's-eye undoing his trouser, but as he went to pull Henry down, a shy yet sudden scream came from the entrance.

"Wait, please. Please no."

Looking quickly Henry saw a boy about his own age stood there with his arms stretched out with a brown envelope his hand.

"Oh god no."

"STOP STRUGGLING."

Bull's-eye looked at the young boy.

"What do you want?"

"I want to buy him please."

"You what? Bull's-eye asked laughing."

"I want to buy him off you please."

Silence fell over them for a moment.

"I have money."

"How much."

"A thousand pounds. You can check it yourself."

Bull's-eye nodded to one of his hench men, to go and look inside the envelope only to find that there was money inside.

One thousand pounds.

Laughing Bull's-eye did up his trousers, turned Henry to face him and gave him a gut punch causing him to collapse to the ground.

"Come on. He's all yours. Fuckin' used goods."

As Ernest watched them leaving, he quickly went to pick Henry up.

"Quickly before they come back."

Marching down the street, Ernest looked back to make sure they weren't coming back.

"Let's hope we get home before they find out it's fake money."

Henry looked at him in shock briefly as they finally got back to Witton Road.

"I'm Ernest."

"I'm Henry."

"Hi."

"Hi."

Weeks passed, and the pair became close. Ernest had surprised his new friend by buying him a silver lighter.

"What's this for?"

"You are my friend. I can buy a gift for my friend."

"Thank you."

The pair looked at each other and smiled.

It was a few nights later when Ernest got out of his bed and made his way to Henry's bed, which was a camper bed in the same room.

"Henry… Hen… Henry?" Ernest whispered as he gently shook his friend and sat on the edge of the bed.

"Ernest? What is it? What's wrong?"

Henry rolled over onto his back as he wiped sleep out of his eyes.

"Could I mean I would like to?"

Henry sat up in bed and gentle stroked Ernest's nervous face. His body was shaking with nervousness and excitement.

"Shhh, it's OK. I was hoping you'd come to me one night. I really like you a lot."

"I really really like you."

Pulling the bed cover back, Ernest crawled in and laid down beside Henry.

"We don't have to if you don't want. I mean, I'm happy to wait. Honestly."

"No, I do want to."

Undressing each other with care as they teased each other, their lips gently touched one another with heat coming off from their naked bodies. Their breathing became slow as Henry carefully kissed and stroked Ernest who laid there only holding Henry's arm.

Wanting him so badly, Henry took Ernest's hand and placed it between his legs and allowed him to fondle him causing him to swell.

Lying down on top of Ernest and breathing upon his neck, he felt Henry kick the bed and cry out in pleasure.

"Please, please I want you inside me," Ernest softly and tenderly spoke as Henry removed Ernest's hand and lifted himself off his new love and knelt on all fours as Ernest knelt behind him.

"Slowly… go slowly, Ernest, please."

"Guiding Ernest inside him, Henry became weak with his eyes closed as Ernest slowly, and at some point, sore for him began to push forward and arch back."

"Oh shit. Er… Ernest… Mmm…"

His mouth opened as Ernest leaned forward holding onto his lover's back, tears began to come from both their eyes, it was almost too much to bear as they became harder until they called out in pleasure when they both finally came.

"No, no. Stay there. Don't come out."

Henry begged as Ernest pushed once more. He finally left Henry and laid down beside him tired and a bit sore. Henry leaned over him and ran his fingers through Ernest's thick black hair as Ernest looked up at him as they kissed once more. Henry took Ernest into his arms, and they finally fell asleep.

It was memories like this that Henry treasured. He came out of his daydream, pulled up his biker jacket collar and carried on with his walk home.

Witton Road

"Come on; you'll have to stay at mine tonight."

"What about Henry? He'll go mad if I'm not there."

Thomas and Ernest came down the path to Thomas's house now on their legs as they leaned up against the garden wall.

Bella had spent almost the entire night sitting in the cold of the living room with a knitted cardigan wrapped around her tiny shoulders, rubbing her hands together to try to keep warm. Voices could be heard from outside making her turn her head with concern.

Knowing she had no choice but to see who it was, Bella walked across the threadbare carpet with bare feet. She could see her own breath pulling the curtains back just enough to have a peak only to have a sudden shock as she saw Thomas and Ernest in such a state.

Opening the front door, Bella called out in a worried and nervous tone of voice as she opened the door and went down the cold steps.

"What the hell happened to you two?"

"There was a fight. Nothing to do with us. We tried to get out but.... As you can see."

"Get inside," Bella ordered as she pushed them up the steps and inside the house.

"OUCH!"

"Be careful."

Bella took such care as she led them into the living room where she cleaned their cuts and bruises.

"Take off your tops."

Removing their tops showed the extent of the fight.

"My goodness I'll have to sort you out, but Ernest my love, Henry goin' to hit the fucking roof."

"We know!" echoed the bloodied men as they sat on the sofa.

"Stay here. I'll go and get some pillows and duvet for Ernest."

"What about Henry?"

Bella always feared Henry never knowing how he was going to be from one minute to the next.

"I'll phone him later. In the meantime, Thomas, go upstairs and wash the blood off your moustaches and stay there."

The spare bedroom was neatly kept and in the summer, a heat trap, but it was ideal for Thomas to sleep as the thought of sharing a bed with Bella in a state did not appeal to him.

The Falklands War had left its mark upon him both physically and mentally.

Maybe Ernest's age or a bit older Thomas had joined the army, which became his family after he was kicked out of his home by his mother.

A heavy drinker and drug-taker and no father to speak of Thomas found friendship in the army, so it was an easy choice when war broke out in the Falklands.

Arriving on the Falklands Island, it was like walking into the hell. Planes coming ever, navy ships being bombed, wounded men waiting to be picked up and taken home, and the horror stories of soldiers being captured.

Thomas knew it was him or them as he fired his gun seeing the bullets flying into the air, and noise is coming from those who got his bullet.

Alongside him were his two best friends Eric who was about twenty-two with the old 1940 glasses and Freddie who was twenty-six and always so happy to hear his own views. They were all like brothers.

But, as the fighting got worse, the three friends pushed forward roaring and shouting to cover of their fear a bomb hit the ground which sent them flying.

Thomas could feel a sharp pain in the back of his leg. He had been wounded. Looking around, he found Freddie lying there not moving.

"FRED!" So much pain shot through him as he pulled himself towards his friend.

"FRED? FREDDIE?" But no reply.

"NO FREDDIE! HELP!"

Thomas had shot up as he heard that cry only to see Eric being taken by Argentina soldiers. Watching his friend been taken against his will, Thomas, attention was broken when other medics came to take him.

"Come on. He's dead mate! We need to get you back to England; otherwise, you'll lose your fucking leg."

"NO! MY FRIENDS ARE BEING TAKEN! He's been taken! ERIC! ERIC!"

Boarding the aircraft, Thomas just watched as he laid on the stretcher still imagining Eric disappearing as the door slammed shut. The plane left the ground, but yet he could hear shapes carrying thousands of men being sunk. Sounds, smells and images of the war will never leave him.

It was weeks later while he was still recovering at Birmingham hospital that he received a letter from Eric's mother that said Eric's body had been found.

It was gut-wrenching as you received a letter from Eric's office that Eric's body had been found. It seemed that the bastards who took him brutally tortured and killed him. The letter never said where or who found him but sudden images of what they did to him would forever haunt him.

He never went to Eric's funeral.

Broken by the touch of a hand, he looked at the window to see a Bella's reflection there was a sense of calm and peace come over him as she let his hand go and left the room.

With an extra blanket under her arm for Ernest, all she could do now was wait for the violent thud at the door.

Chapter 5
Separation

The morning sun was just that bit warmer as David made his way to Thomas's house. Knocking on the door, he noticed how quiet the street was. For a change, only the odd person made their way to the news agents no doubt to pick up the Sunday newspaper.

Bella had told Ernest to lock the door if he wanted to get changed, but the pain seemed worse when he moved. Thomas was sitting at the kitchen table rubbing his forehead which was still badly bruised and the cut lips sore. At least his nose had stopped bleeding.

"Morning, David." The sound of relief came from Bella's voice. She felt it could be Henry who had always made her feel nervous.

"Morning, Bella. Where is he then?"

"Just in the kitchen."

Shutting the door and touching her bottom lip, she followed David to the kitchen. As she walked past the living room, she heard the lock go on.

"BLOODY HELL! HA, HA… what the fuck happened to you?"

David could not help but laugh at him as Thomas sat back in his chair looking up from under his hand which shaded his sore eyes.

"We went to the other pub last night."

"With who? Who's we."

"Ernest and me."

"Ernest! Shit. Henry going to love this."

"Yeah, well, I'll deal with that when he comes. OK."

Thudding could be held from the kitchen as the door was hit hard by a fist.

"We're about to find out now. Aren't we?"

Fear caused Thomas to go white and feel sick to his stomach.

"Hide anything sharp," Thomas quickly reacted to his own suggestion as he looked around but not moving from his chair.

"It's the fuckin belt buckle that hurts ya. Watch out for that instead."

Henry stood at the door seeming to be calm with a fag between his fingers which he dropped as Bella open the door with fear.

She dared get in his way as he pushed passed her and strolled over to the kitchen. As he went in, he turned to see Thomas now sitting straight in the chair, palms flat on the table as David was sitting casually not really caring that Henry was standing right behind him.

"What the bloody hell happened to you? Where's Ernest."

"We went to small Heath"

"What the fuck for? What's wrong with our normal haunt?"

Fuming, Thomas jumped quickly and walked towards the sink holding on to the edge of it to try to calm himself. Thomas locked out the window as he answered the question.

"Because we are both sick of you two goin' for each other!"

Silence fell for a moment as Henry scanned the room.

"What happened?" Henry's voice became sharp as Ernest had not come home last night.

"We were at the Garrison just having a few. A fight broke out. We went to get up to leave, but we got caught up in it. I got a black. I cut lips and a bleeding nose, but Ernest."

A worried look came across Henry's face which was sick, looking pale, and was fearful.

"What about Ernest?"

David moves away and headed towards the corner cupboard.

"He came off worse. I brought him back here."

Henry walked closure with his eyes piercing.

"Where is he?"

"In the living room, but! He doesn't want to see you. Not yet anyway."

Anger grew fast from deep inside as Henry stood even nearer to the table, Bella was in the doorway and David now found himself looking for a knife.

Pushing passed Bella causing her to nearly fall backwards, Henry went to the living room door and try to open it, but it was locked from the inside.

"Ernest, Ernest, open the door and let me be with you, please. Ernest?"

But no reply.

"ERNEST! OPEN THE FUCKING DOOR."

"No."

A quiet voice came from inside.

"No, Henry. I can't. I can't let you see me like this. Please leave me alone."

Henry slammed his forehead against the door in excruciating pain. He slammed his fist hard into the door screaming loud enough that silence fell from inside the kitchen. No one moved nor spoke as his pain was too much to bear.

Later, Thomas started to talk to cover up for his heartbroken friend.

"So?" Moving away from the sink and back to his chair, Thomas sat back down inviting David to rejoin him.

"What are you doing with your bookmaking? I'm paying rent on a room and don't forget. A room that's not being used at all. So! What are you playing at?"

"ALRIGHT! I'll fucking use it. OK."

"When?"

"Next week."

"No, I don't think so, sunshine. This week."

"That's what I meant!"

David turned his head to see Henry who walked past him and stood behind Thomas.

"Get an eye full of this."

Taking a paper bag out of his jacket pocket he threw it across the table at Thomas who just look down at it for a moment feeling Henry walking up from behind him it causes him to shudder.

Snatching it off the table, Thomas pulled out notes.

Money. Some fifty thousand pounds.

"Where did you get all this from?"

Concern showed upon his face for a moment as Bella left the room Henrys' eyes followed her.

"Let's just say it was something that she begged me for. And I mean beg."

"Well, that's your business not ours now about the bookmarking."

"I changed my mind."

Henry suddenly found his voice and was in no mood to mess around.

"For fuck's sake, David! You just said this week."

"Ernest has got the little notebook with all the names in it."

"DON'T! You fuckin' move," Thomas pointed at Henry who nearly walked off towards the door.

"BELLA!" Thomas had felt Henry go to move as he called Bella back into the kitchen.

"What is it, Thomas?" Bella seemed fed up as she never got any time to herself, and also being in view of Henry frightened her.

"Don't come here with a fucking attitude. Go to the living room and ask Ernest for the notebook and the money that he hides under his cardigan. We're off to the pub; meet us there."

"Fine, whatever."

Henry was now gripping the back of the chair as she went to the door a quick glance towards the kitchen in case Henry came out without warning.

The warmth of the sun had been taken by a cold wind that swift up the street and took your breath away.

As they got to the pub it was peaceful and calm, only a few men followed from behind them as they say a coal fire.

"This is where things get interesting, David."

"Um?"

"Up you go." Thomas's eyes went towards the bar.

"No chance."

"You."

"I'll go." Henry pushed in just as Thomas started to lose it a bit.

"No, you won't, our kid. You've paid enough out for I'm. I'll fucking go. What do you want?"

"I'll have a small whisky."

"Henry? You never touch the stuff."

"Well, I fuckin' need it now."

"Fair enough. David?"

"A pint."

Leaving his two young friends to get the order, Henry sat down with one leg resting across the other looking down at the floor not saying a word for at least five minutes until David thought he'd be clever to make a remark at Henry.

"Listen yeah, Ernest fine," David's sarcastic remark never got a reply.

"Here we go, lads."

The round wooden tray had not landed on the table when Henry took his whisky and knocked it and slammed the empty glass down taking cigarettes and lighter from his trouser pocket. David watched and as the cigarette hit the table. He stretched across to take a fag.

Henry just watched.

"Give us ya lighter."

"Great a fuckin' job."

"Here!" Thomas interrupted and handed David a box of swan matches.

"And listen, listen, yeah? We need a runner and a taker as well as something to listen to for results."

"A radio, I'll be a runner," Henry answered quietly as Thomas Lent in.

"Ernest will be better within a week. He could be our little taker."

Henry knew that if he reacted to David's remarks, it would end up in a fight, and in his mood, it could be deadly.

Wiping the bits of tobacco off his trouser leg, he said, "I could be a runner," Thomas asked as he turned to look at Henry.

"You? Fuck me. I'm only twenty-two and run faster than you."

"I'm only thirty-eight. Alright. Alright. I'll be a taker."

"Again Ernest is twenty-one and run faster."

"Cheeky bastard."

The door was opened very slowly, and the sound of high heels could be heard as Bella made her way towards the table where Thomas was sitting, fully where those eyes were on her from the men that had surrounded the bar.

"Did you get it?" David called out in an ice-cold tone of voice.

"Yes. Here." Bella handed the Notebook and the small plastic bag which contain the money.

"Thank you."

"Ernest alright then?"

Bella nearly choked as Henry threw the question at her.

"He asked me to give you this."

Looking over his shoulder, Bella handed him an envelope. Taking it between his forefinger and middle finger, he held it as he finished his fag.

"Good night. See you back home? Thomas?"

"Yeah, alright then," Bella answered quietly as she turn to work away but yet was teased by two men, and they grabbed her arm and pulled her into his big rock-hard gut as the other stood right up from behind her playing with her long black hair, but their laughter was too loud to cover her cries to make them stop.

"LEAVE HER ALONE!" He had heard enough as Thomas finally jumped up out of his chair bellowing out so loud that even Henry jumped out of his skin.

Spitting as he screamed out the man finally shoved her causing her to step quickly over herself.

"It was just a bit of fun mate."

The fat slope spoke through his broken teeth.

"A bit of rough; ha ha; she was always up for a quick fuck," His mate spoke as he laughs making his way back to the bar not really caring for their comments. Thomas watched out the window as Bella moved passed quickly and finally disappeared before sitting himself back down, he went back to looking through the notebook. David just sat there. Henry had opened the envelope and begin to read it to himself.

It was from Ernest.

To my dearest loving Henry.
Please don't be angry at me. You must understand that I am not looking you out just to be cruel but to take time that I need to get better and be away from you for a moment. I cannot longer listen to those who you have slept with boost about you and then not those that look you up and down even if I do understand why they do as you are very handsome with your blond hair and

blue eyes. Me? I'm far from good looking, but please know that I do love you. I really love you. I will see you once I feel better.

**All my love,
Your Ernest X**

That was enough if not too much as Henry felt a dagger rammed into his heart. This was too much so his only other opinion was to sleep in an empty cold bed at home.

He folded up the letter and placed it back into its ribbed envelope.

"Love letter?" David asked, and Henry refused to answer as he put the letter into his trouser pocket blazing the cigarette between his lips and lit it. Smoke came from his nose as a warning to not push him.

Right, so what day can we make a start?

Breaking the silence as he always did to stop his two young friends from killing each other.

"May as well start tomorrow morning." Henry gazed up from his cigarette.

"But it's fucking Sunday. You never heard of a lye in."

"You have a fucking lie in every passing day!"

Thomas got in there as soon as he could.

"It's settled then! Thomas morning. We can spend the day getting everything in yes!" David never answered.

"That's fine with me. It's not like I've got anyone worth staying up for."

David gave a pathetic sigh tipping his head down chin nearly touching his chest.

Just enough daylight remained as it shone on the pavement that they could make their way home.

"Night, you two."

"Night, David."

Cutting away from his friends, David walked across the road and made his way home.

Making their way home, Thomas saw that something was wrong with Henry but dare not ask.

"Hello!" Voices came from behind them.

Turning to see who it was, they could see a young man no more than early twenties quickly walking to catch them up.

"What does he want?"

Henry shrugged his broad shoulders to Thomas's question.

At last, catching them up, the young man took Henry by his elbow and looked into Henry's eyes as though he was meant to know what he wanted.

"I, um, I was wondering if I could see you? Tonight?" Thomas watched on in shock not believing what he was seeing. Ernest was always the one, wasn't he?

"Do you want me to go? Henry? Are you coming? Ernest will be there."

"Yes, but he doesn't want to see me. Does he?" Pulling Henry aside for a moment. Thomas forced Henry to look at him.

"OI! What the fuck are ya playing at? Hay? What about Ernest? Um? Don't you think he feels insecure at the best of times when it comes to you? I mean, you are his world."

"That's why he's locked me out. Don't you think that I don't know how he feels? How much fuckin' pain I get in when he's not close."

"Then don't do what I think you are thinking about."

The moment passed as he watched Henry's eyes fill up with tears as he looked away.

"Where do you live?"

"Henry? No."

The young man pointed down the street.

"Endecott road."

"Alone?"

"Yes."

Thomas went into shock and worried about what he was going to say to Ernest.

"Night, Thomas."

"You striped bastard."

In hope that he could stop Henry from making a mistake, he did what he did best. Full fist straight into his friend's face causing him to fall to the floor out cold.

"Now then up, you come."

Throwing Henry over his shoulder, Thomas looked at the young man who stood in shock.

"Yes? Go on. Fuck off and off to bed we go."

Thomas walked down the street and round the corner.

The house was in darkness apart from the kitchen light.

"Bella?"

"No, only me," Ernest answered as he came out of the kitchen and down the hallway.

"Shhh…"

"Thomas? What happened? What did you do to Henry?"

"Knocked him out. Long story short. A young fella took a fancy to him and tempted him back to his place."

"And?"

"He nearly… NEARLY. I will stress that, but I knocked him out."

Ernest gentle touched Henry's leg as though he knew how close he came to losing him.

"He's going to sleep upstairs, excuse me, but he's heavy."

Ernest watched as Thomas walk off with his only love dangling over of his shoulder.

"No, wait."

"What now?" Thomas spoke in exasperation.

"Bring him in here."

"But you said. You just said."

"Just please."

Rolling his eyes, Thomas made his way into the living room and carefully dropped Henry on the sofa.

"Night, you two."

"Night."

Closing the door, Ernest undressed Henry and crawled onto the sofa finally covering them up.

Bella had gone straight to sleep as Thomas finally caught up straight quickly opened the door to the bedroom silently so as not to wake her, she had slept.

Walking in on tip toes he went over to the bed to look at her.

A beautiful young woman with dark skin, long brown hair, full figure, and the biggest brown eyes he had ever seen.

How could such a beautiful creature have any such feelings for a drunken, violent man, but she did. Not wanting to wake her he left the room and closed the door.

The spare room at the end of the corridor was always made up in case someone needed it.

"It'll do," before walking in, Thomas paused and looked back the landing where Bella was.

"Good night, sweet angel."

Walking inside, Thomas got undressed and crawled into a bed which felt cold and lonely covering himself up fixed at the window and hopefully fall asleep.

Henry slowly came around with the feeling of someone on top of him slowly opening up his eyes. He saw Ernest just looking at him.

"Thomas hit ya 'coz you were goin' to go off."

Wrapping one arm around Ernest's waist, he rubbed his eyes.

"I know."

"Why? Why? I thought we were past all that".

"Because of your letter."

"Oh no. Don't blame me for what you nearly did."

"Right, that's it."

Pushing Ernest flat onto his back, Henry pinned him down as he sat on top of him.

"Do you have any idea what that fuckin' letter did to me? You nearly killed me."

"But would you have gone off if Thomas hadn't stopped you?"

"No. Because I love you. I love you so much. And … and the very thought of you not being near me or with me kills me."

The pair looked at one another as Henry carefully bent down to kiss Ernest.

"We can't. Not with these bruises."

Looking Ernest up and down, he finally released him, and as he laid down, Henry pulled Ernest into him so close as he stroked his Love hair.

"I don't want to leave you, Henry. I want to be with you. Always please keep me with you."

"I will. I'll keep you close to me and never let you go. Never."

The ice-cold rain finally came down bouncing off the window sills as they fell asleep with a tight grip on each other.

Chapter 6
David's Flat

Henry arrived at the back of the building Ernest leaving to sleep and rest. He got there half an hour before Thomas turned up no sign of David.

"Morning, our kid."

"Morning," Henry answered as he turned to look over his shoulder as he sat on the bottom of the iron staircase smoking the cigarette that was gently placed at the corner of his mouth.

Thomas looked different clean, cleaner than normal his face washed and shaved apart from his moustache but his hair! Henry could not tell as he still had his fake leather cap on.

"Sorry about ... you know."

"Oh what? This?" Henry pointed at his right cheek which was a bit swollen black and green.

"Yeah, that."

"Don't worry about it." Henry gave out a sigh before he continued.

"I am glad you did."

"You are?"

"Coz if you didn't I may and I stressed that word may have gone off. And if it had of been David or anyone else I'd of killed 'em."

"Comforting, but you're welcome."

Scanning the small alleyway, it was obvious that they were one down.

"Where is he then?"

"Christ knows. I've been since 7:30 and no sign yet."

"For fuck sake, I said 8:00 in the morning. You heard me say 8 am!"

"Shhh... shut it. People will fuckin' hear you."

"Right, come on." Thomas turned when Henry stopped him.

"We'll give him five more minutes. If he doesn't show up, then we'll go and get him," Henry said as he got up.

"What is it? Why are you looking at me?" Thomas asked in a worried tone.

"You're clean."

"You sayin' I'm dirty."

"No, well, yeah at times, but you look different."

"Yeah well, I'm trying a new look," shuffling his coat collar twitching his neck.

"Mr. Hyde coming out?" Henry said as he knew that just like himself Thomas had a split personality.

"No."

"You try doing something with that cap of yours."

"Nothing wrong with this cap. It's just well warm. That's all. Fuck off."

Henry just gave a friendly smile.

"Five minutes is up. David's place."

He'll be in bed. Nine times out of ten that's where he normally is.

We'll go and get him up.

The slow walk back to Witton Road was silent. Smoking, the odd cough and sniffing, not a word was spoken between the two men even though they had so much to talk about, some of the past and what was happening in their love lives, but that sense of stiff upper lip stuck as well as shame.

"No need to tell him he doesn't need to know."

Talking inside his head, Thomas looked over the road while Henry still had his hand inside his pockets one which head Ernest friendship card.

Small but worn as it was part of the gift, he had given Henry some time ago. The lighter gripping it every time he put his hand in his pocket.

Witton road was quite although people were up there no sign of them out in the streets. Thomas went up the stairs first as Henry followed him through the main entrance to the block of flats.

The flat door was locked, and the bell did not work, and the knocker was wobbly, so Thomas used his fist banging on the door, but no answer.

Stood there looked up and down the corridor only to see Mrs Mackay coming up the staircase. She was small and around old lady but a force of nature.

"You boys, alright?"

Thomas and Henry just give a small smile.

"Is he in?"

"Yeah, he's in but unlike normal people lie in the lazy bastard."

Her remarks made Henry chuckle.

"That boy needs kicking into shape."

"Don't worry, Mrs Mackay. Henry and me will see to that."

Mrs Mackay just gave a grunt and continued on her way.

As they stood either side of the door, Thomas tried one more time only a lot louder banging on the door but no response still.

"Fuck it." Lifting a face, Thomas got ready to smash it in, but Henry pushed his left down and stored in between his old friend and the door. He pulled out a pocketknife forcing in between the gap of the door and the lock he forced it, finally opening it.

"Er? Where did you learn that?"

"Don't ask."

As they walk inside the flat, there was a smell of body odour was strong. Curtains not pulled back were torn and dirty. Walking into the small living room they could not help but notice the torn carpet beneath their feet.

"I mean… Come on. I go to work. You and Ernest go to work. But you don't live like fuckin' pigs."

Thomas could not help but comment, always proud of his working-class background as was Henry and Ernest. They always took pride in their homes.

"Yeah, well. He had coffee to work plenty of times. I mean George has offered him a cleaning job, and he got all fucking snobby and said that cleaning was below him."

"Well, Henry, I think this is below anyone what we see here let's go and get the sod up. Don't look at the kitchen. Do you need the bag?" Thomas asked with a giggle.

"NO!"

The bed was a single one. Sheets nearly off the bed. The duvet barely covered David's thin body and the mattress needed throwing away.

"Sleeping beauty?"

"In his fucking dreams bright, let's get him up," Henry remarked.

"Shh… you get that, and I'll get this, and on three. We tip it." Thomas ordered as Henry got the head end and they gripped under the mattress Thomas counted then nodded for Henry and himself to tip.

Quick enough David rolled over fast and hit the floor as they dropped the mattress back down.

"Get up, you lazy bastard. I said 8:00! 8:00."

Thomas bellowed out like an army officer painting at David as he woke up yelling that he'd hurt himself.

"We'll wait outside. GET DRESSED!"

Pulling the door, Thomas and Henry sat on the staircase.

"So?"

Thomas had noticed a slight change in Henry lately even more so when it involved Ernest.

"So? What?"

"What happened between you and Ernest? Last night? And no details thank you."

Shrugging his shoulders, Henry looked down at his feet, then back at Thomas.

"Nothing."

"Nothing? You were not in the mood? Or he didn't do it for you? What?"

"No," Henry stood up and lent against the banister. Thomas followed.

"I woke up, and Ernest was looking after me. He was just so loving and caring, and I just… I felt you know I couldn't get caressed. Nothing."

Thomas could see that Henry was feeling insecure as if feared he would lose Ernest.

"It's him. It's just how Ernest loves you so so much. He told me."

Warm tears built up in Henry's eyes and rolled down his cheeks.

"And I love him, Thomas. I really love him so much that it hurts at times, and it kills me to think that I might want too much of him. Not saying too much but we do make love. But, last night, all I wanted to do was just hold him. Hold him in my arms and fall asleep."

"Then why? God, why? Don't you tell him this. Any fucking dick can see that you're Ernests' world. And sex? well sex isn't everything. When I first met Bella I took her in. Yes, I will admit I knew what she was and when we had sex, sometimes back now, I didn't love her. But just lately I… I just want to cuddle her. Love her. Make her happy. She is so beautiful so perfect and for someone like me...' Thomas removed his cab to reveal his bald head with grey hair around the edges."

"I know that Bella doesn't love me. I know that always have. But you two have something that is so special that you should be protective of it."

"I don't…" Henry feared for Ernest not himself.

The four of them had built up a reputation for fighting, house break in always David's hobby and going warfare, which gave them the nickname the Brummie boys of Aston, which made Henry and Ernest relationship at target as well as what people would say.

"Now you just listen to me you stupid bastard. Don't give a fuck what people say or think you and him are the only two people who need to know how you both feel about each other and that is all that matters."

Wiping his eyes on the palm of his hands and rubbing his nose on his selves, Henry just smiled. "Listen our kid. Go." You and Ernest go to Aston Park for a picnic or lunch. Hold hands and kiss if you want to. I am in. Let's be honest, babe. You already know for outburst of violence no one is going to say anything to you okay.

"No. We've got work half the time."

"Then get time off. I'll cover. I'll help George. Just show Ernest what he means to you. I should have done that with our Bella."

The door to David's flat started to open making them look over quickly.

"Go downstairs, get some fresh air. Go."

Henry turned and made his downstairs hearing Thomas shouting a David who was already geared up for a fight, most of it frustration.

Outside Henry stood in the car park taking deep breaths and dried his eyes.

The main door was thrown open as Thomas stormed out in a rage with David being shoved.

Part 2

In his back, out into the car park, Henry looked at him up and down as he was finally back in his baggy jeans and denim jacket, but his combat laces weren't tied up correctly.

"We agreed eight o'clock and that you cannot get that right?" shouted Thomas. He pushed David making him wobble sideways.

"Henry! You go and see if you can get your hands on a black board?"

Thomas had put himself in between David and Henry never knowing who would snap first.

"George has been outback. We used it when we had a darts team. I'll ask, see if he still has one."

"Good. I'll go to the butcher get my portable radio. And you…." Pointing his middle finger into David chest.

"OUCH! What!"

"Go and find a table."

"Where am I meant to find the fucking table?"

"Look for one. Someone might have one on the street going free."

As the three left each other, Henry made his way to the pub.

"Err… our kid."

George handed him the black board from inside the cellar where it had been kept for too long.

"Ta."

"Hey. Box of chalk."

George pulled out a small box of white chalk and handed it to Henry who stuffed it in his back pocket.

"You still don't have the rubber to the board? Sorry mate."

"No, no problem. I'll just go and get it that's if the wife hasn't moved it."

Henry smiled as George went off, he checked his jacket pockets. He could still fill the little card from Ernest in there he never had no intension of throwing it away.

Putting the black board long ways under his arm George come back quickly and handed him the thick black board rubber it looked as if it had come from the classroom.

"Err, babs."

"Ta."

Watching Henry sort himself out George had serious concerns about what he was doing he had known Henry since he started working there at the age of eighteen now twenty-two, he still sees a child which is nickname for him was baby face.

"Have you seen Ernest today?"

"Only this morning; otherwise no," quick and sharp answer as he got ready to leave.

George got the door and watched him leave but not without some friendly advice.

"Be careful babs, yeah. For god's sake because if the cops catch you. You will end up in prison for months as we as a big fat fine."

"Don't worry George I'll be careful."

But leaving, George watched the young man go down the yard though the wooden gate and down the back alleyway.

The butchers were steady for once, with the day off Thomas walked in but not without saying morning to everyone as he went up to Norman who had his son helping him for once as it wasn't often that he ever helped his father his attitude was Thomas will do it. I just want the business.

"Morning, Norman!"

"Morning, son. How can I help ya? What you do in here on day off?"

"Just wondering if I could pick up my little radio out back? Bella has got me re-decorating the kitchen and I need something decent to listen to, if that's OK?"

"'Course it is, son, help yourself."

"Tar."

The preparation room was not as clear or tidy as it was when he was in.

The chopping board had not been washed, tops not wiped down, knives either left out on the side dangerously close to the edge or still not washed with blood still on them and no sign of washing up. Liquid in the sink and blood covered clothes.

"I don't have time to clean up. Norman. Norman," Tut-tutting as he quickly locked around the room.

"You really need to kick that lad into shape."

Finding the radio under a dish cloth. Thomas unplugged it rolled the wire round it and pushed the aired down he tucked it under his arm and walked out nearly slipping on the floor.

"Cheers Norm! See you in the morning!"

"AR! Bye Thomas!"

Closing the door on his way out he could see some of his customers making their way to Normans many of them elderly ladies who gave a wave saying good morning to them and only if forced stopped to chat with them although he could really do without it at the moment.

Despite his cruel past Thomas was well liked by the ladies especially when he gives them the best cuts of lamb, beef or pork.

"Er... babs... let me help ya," Thomas saw Henry with a blackboard making his way up the staircase.

"Thank you."

Lifting it up between them they climbed up the iron steps of just ten steps.

Open the door they were far from shocked when David was nowhere to be seen.

"Maybe he actually made the effort and got the table book of using own intuition?"

Thomas tried to cover up for David.

"No. Don't be stupid he's fucked off again!"

As they went further in they heard snoring in the corner and to their surprise there he was.

David was sat in a chair, feet upon on a small stool and his cap over his eyes, curled up looking cosy.

"OI!" Thomas dropped the board without warning Henry who still had his grip on it. Taking care not to fall over the debris on the floor Thomas put his foot on the chair leg supporters are brutally kick them making David legs hit the floor holding his cap.

"Where's the fucking table?"

David tries to sort himself out as he looked up only to see a furious Thomas with his arms out wide.

"I've got it!"

"Unless it's a fucking invisible table? I can't fucking see it!"

"A woman had one on the street for free I told her that I'd take it and my mates will pick it up later."

"You said WHAT?"

Henry could not resist making a comment towards Thomas.

"Hyde's making an appearance now."

"Fuck off, our kid."

Focusing back on David who had a smug look upon his face he put the radio on the stool and grabbed David by his upper arm nearly piercing skin with his short razor nails.

"Get up. Come on."

He pushed David out the door as fast as he could.

Henry watched.

"What am I meant to do with the board?"

"Just put it up the best you can we won't be long."

Slamming the door behind them, Henry just looked around without noticing that his grip was lose dropping the blackboard and rubber on to the floor causing him to look down.

"Ohh, for fuck's sake!"

The walk back to the market which, was not that far from where the woman had left the table outside her shop gave sign of relief for Thomas. At least it was not too far away from the building they had just left.

"How fucking hard is it get someone to help with moving it?"

"Shut your mouth!"

Very slowly was Thomas running out of patience with David as it was one thing that he refused to work but this was taking the piss as it was his idea after all and yet his heart was not it.

"I've heard enough of this listen to me you stupid bastard. Henry and me are putting our necks on the line for you with extra work now as Ernest isn't well so pull your finger out!"

Deep anger showed itself as he had been shown up in public. David had a reputation to a hold and felt that he had no choice but to threaten he is older the friend.

"If you ever touch me like that again? I'll cut of your other three fingers! Alright!"

Stomping off like a teenager not helped by his fashion, David went off but what is soon come back for now.

The table was just outside the shop only a dining table made of wood but would do for what they need it for and big enough to spread out the racing papers.

"Get that end. You can walk at the fucking front," Thomas ordered as the gripped it and from under the table where they could feel that they hoped was chewing gum not snot.

Picking it up, Thomas forced it into David's back.

"Move!"

David's face was filled with frustration as they made their way out of the market and into the streets.

The table took up most of any space in the streets as they wobbled through having to stop every so often to put it down to try to get a better grip but for Thomas, three fingers missing of one hand was not making it easy as they continue down the street.

Laughs and crude comments were being thrown out towards Thomas mostly.

"That for Bella?"

"She goin' on top of it!?"

"No mate he'll have her ever it begins him for it!" Despite the sick remarks, Thomas refused to react. It was not worth it, that and also did not went to draw attention to himself or David.

Taking care not to break his neck, they walk it down the alley way and with one step at a time made, they went up the iron staircase with the door already open.

Forcing it through the door and hearing it scratching against the door frame, David's foul mouth became louder.

"Fuck this." Dropping it to the floor and walked off leaving Thomas outside.

"OI! You bastard!"

"Fuck you!"

Squeezing himself between the frame while breathing in as much as he could he finally got inside and decided to Drag it in.

"Not that I want to be an asshole or anything, but can someone give me a hand with this fucking table please?" still trying to pull it in.

Henry just finished putting the black board on the wall with a power drill borrowed from a mate with a fag hanging outside of his mouth watched his footing as he climbed down from the stool and walked over to Thomas.

"Thank you, son."

Henry walked past his friend and squeezed himself outside taking the other hand of the table they finally lifted it and walked in with it on its side.

"Where do you want it?" asked with his fag still in his mouth Henry turned clockwise to go near the blackboard.

"Just here drop it."

Slamming it down Thomas checked his hands for cuts when wiping his hands on his coat and removing his cap to dap his forehead, giving David a stare.

It had not even started up and it was becoming even more noticeable that David did not seem to be bothered by this idea which was not normal given his past attempt to earn money.

"We're nearly there I think?" Thomas stood in the middle of the room examining it. Henry sat on the table watching David carefully.

"We need the evening papers and the Birmingham papers for the racing results note pads for betting slips."

Henry told his two friends as he tapped on the table and prayed that they didn't get caught.

"And bets."

"You've woken up then?"

Thomas spoke as he lent against the table next to Henry facing David who had sat back down on the chair.

"What about the pub?"

Henry gave a frame stare directly at David who generally that was a clever thing to say.

"No."

"Why not? News travelled around quicker there. I am not putting George's livelihood in danger because you went to make it easy for yourself."

"Fine the butcher?"

"Don't take the piss. We sell meat not bets. Anyway, it's old ladies that come in okay, yes at times I see them go towards the beating shop that's coz it's legal."

"Well then, you two think of something," frustrated by the lack of help David got up out of the chair and pounded he floor as he started to pass up and down.

Henry could not take David's attitude when he was like this and it was either hit him or talk to Thomas so Henry made his way towards him.

"Look, there are men out there who love to gamble but dare in fear that their wives or girlfriends caught 'em."

"And."

"They'd be more than happy to come somewhere where there is no questions asked spend what they want and keep their winnings to themselves."

Thomas new what Henry was talking of as these sorts of men would be easy targets quick and easy. Addicted to gambling.

"The pub then?" Thomas said as he gave a smile as he placed his hand on the back of Henry's neck.

Letting out a deep sigh with smoke coming down his nostrils, Henry knew this would have to be kept out of George's ear shot if he found out it would not only cost Henry his job but Georges' license.

"There's an old lady called Mrs Wilson. She loves a little bet there, and she might give it a go."

Henry never answered as he took his fag out of his lips and handed it to Thomas who smiled and took it from him and finished it off.

Taking the long walk home, they left the building and made their way out of town, heads down and coat collars pulled up they never spoke a word to each other past other people. Men making their way home, women picking up their children from school or elderly couples taking in the evening air.

"I'm off the pub."

"Fine," Thomas answered silently.

David's stopped to cross over leaving them both to go off.

"OI!" Thomas stopped for a moment as called out quickly just as David crossed over.

"What?"

"See you tomorrow evening at six!"

David just grunted and threw his arms up in the air if he really did not care.

"Come on, Thomas, leave him."

Witton road seemed a bit busy as cars went by Henry and Thomas would give a wave to those they knew.

"You are going back home? Or do you went to come back with me?"

"No, I'll go home have something to eat then bed. You?"

"Bella's cooked faggots, mash and peas with gravy. Tell you but why don't you come and have tea with us? Ernest hasn't seen you all day."

Henry suddenly stopped dead and looked up the street as much as he wanted to see Ernest, he knew that he really wasn't in the mood for Henry to be near. He had made that clear last night.

"What? Bella won't mind her romantic meal being distributed?"

"No fucking chance of that. Look, if Ernest has locked you out of the living room? You can have the fold down bed. In the hallway."

"What's wrong with the spare bedroom?"

"I'm in it," Thomas looked far from happy when he announced it as Henry never answered it. Too much of a sensitive subject.

"Babs, let's get home."

Pulling Henry's arm they finally got home.

To the smell of home cooking, clothes had been washed were hanging over the heaters and the smell of bleach.

"Bella! Henry's having some tea and staying the night so an extra plate and the camper bed is needed!" Thomas ordered as he went into the camper bed under the stairs Henry tried the living room door. Looked only a note.

> "Henry, I'm still sore, need Some time to myself still. But please don't be mad at me as I love you so much."
> All yours
> Ernest x

Henry felt his blood boil deep inside him and the pain was too much but he dare not show any emotion, he folded it up and put it inside his pocket.

"Give us a hand, our kid."

Henry helped pull the bed out and the pair opened it up close up against the living room door not knowing that Ernest was listening at the door.

Sat at the table sharing the gravy jug between them. Thomas put some on Bella's dinner as he could hear her moving around upstairs.

"Do you fancy a Whiskey? It's Johnnie Walker."

"Go on then."

Grabbing two whisky glasses, he commenced to fill them up and put his down near his plate and handed Henry his.

"Ta."

"Not a problem, Bella!"

Bella had finally come downstair with pillows and duvet all made up in her arms and dumped it on the camper bed and set it up for Henry, she could not believe who this was for, this must be hard for them but for Henry even more as she would have to tell Ernest this even if he didn't believe her the bed was proof.

Placing the pillows and unfolding the duvet, she drew the hallway curtains and the front door.

Finally at the kitchen where Thomas and Henry were really getting their food down their throats and having their drinks to swill it down, she suddenly noticed that one was missing.

"Where's David?"

"Pub," Thomas replied with a full stomach and finishing off his whisky.

No one spoke a word as they mopped up the gravy with bread much to Bella's delight a sense of pride and Thomas enjoyed her cooking but would never tell her.

Henry finished at last and got up to clear the table.

"I can do that. Henry?"

"It's alright, Bella. I don't mind."

As Henry filled the sink, he threw a dish towel at Thomas who took a yawn when the towel landed on his face.

"You can dry."

Bella just smiled and put it in her pocket as she got up to go into the garden to look at her flowers she was growing.

The evening seemed warmer than normal with the kitchen clean Bella sat at the table reading a book that she had problems getting through.

Going to school was not really an option because of her skin colour but also her mother never put her into School.

The only chance to learn was on her box bedroom teaching herself to read and write while her mother was being paid by a wealthy man to pleasure him.

The sounds of which haunted her as a child until she become a teenager that he had turned his attention to her but if she had refused him, the outcome would be extreme.

Henry and Thomas sat outside in the backyard with the money box and notepad between them so that no one could see it.

"Right! Let's see what we have here."

Thomas handed the book to Henry as he counted it out of what was owed and what people had lost.

Chapter 7
Witton Road

"Here you are, Mrs Pickles, four sausages and half a pound of pig's liver."

Thomas wrapped the meat up for the elderly lady who must be in her nineties. He went around to the outside of the counter and put it in her trolley.

It was quite nothing unusual for a Monday morning. Norman had been quiet most of the morning with a worrying look on his face.

"Norman? You OK?"

"Umm."

"You seem quite this morning. Everything alright?"

Norman was gazing over the produce to see if anything needed topping up.

"Ohh, I'm sorry, Thomas. I... I'm so sorry and ashamed of what you saw last week. I keep saying that boy of mine to clean up, but he doesn't listen. He wants the business, but not all the hard work that goes with it."

"You need to kick that into shape or else he will run this place down into the ground."

He was feeling sorry for his boss. He was a good man, but Thomas also knew that his son and wife were all about money and never willing to help.

He did start the business from scratch. He inherited it from his father.

He didn't answer him and went to put the kettle on. The little doorbell rang.

"Good morning, Mrs Wilson. What can I do for you?"

The lady in her eighties asked Thomas to come on the other side of the counter where she was standing.

"What's wrong, Mrs Wilson? You alright? Do you want me to call your daughter?"

"No, I'm fine. Look. Come here; look…."

She took out ten pounds from her handbag and handed it to Thomas. He looked at her confused.

"Ten pounds on black thunder, the 2.40 pm race. Tomorrow 5/1."

"Mrs Wilson, I don't know."

"Yes, you do know what I mean, I saw young Henry and he said to give it to you."

Reluctantly, he took the money and put it into his back pocket. He took a piece of paper from the till role to write and signed it before handing it to his favourite customer.

"If I win, we'll go half and half again." Tapping her nose she finally went to leave. Norman came out from the backroom.

"Good day, Norman!"

"Good day, Mrs Wilson!"

With the betting money in his back pocket, Thomas went back behind the counter as Norman handed over his cup of tea.

"Cheers, Thomas."

"Cheers."

The afternoon was quiet and slow. George had gone off for lunch leaving Henry alone behind the bar.

Most of those in the power were either on the date or just finished their shifts at the factories.

Jeff, who did not come very often had decided to pop in on his way home.

Jeff came with his brown curly hair, short stature and tanned skin from his time spent in Thailand where he had met his wife some years ago.

"A pint please, Henry."

"Right."

Henry pulled the pint but could not help but notice how Jeff looked worried brushing his dirty face with his hands.

"You alright?"

"No. Not really, son."

"Why?"

Henry stood nearby and lent on the bar looking towards the front door to check anyone coming in but lent to the side to hear what Jeff was saying as Jeff put his pint down.

"It's my wife. I want to put a bet on and lost thirty pounds in a bet. That's all. Nothing bad, and now she is found out, so I can't tell any lies as she'll know. The cow checks my Pocket and now! Now…

"She's found all the bookies and told them to kick me out! I tell you what Henry stay away from women."

"Don't worry about that. I am not a fan of females."

"Oh shit, forgot. Sorry."

Henry went quiet for a moment looking down at the floor.

"You still want to bet?"

"Of course, I do. But how?"

"What if I told you about a place where people go to put a bet on? No matter how much they want, no one knows about it. Knows where it is."

Jeff's interest had been pricked as he looked up from his pint glass.

"You mean illegal like!"

"If you want to call it that. But, if you have control of what you spend, your wife will never know."

"Where is it?"

Henry took a piece of paper from the till roll and wrote the address down.

"Do you know the people?"

"I do. Here."

Pushing towards him, Jeff checked around before picking it up.

"It's above the abandoned shop just off the main street."

"If I win?"

"If you win they will come and tell you. You can go and collect your winnings."

"And if I lose."

"It you lose, that's your problem not mine."

"Fair enough. I don't know."

Henry took the paper away from Jeff and tried to burn it using his silver lighter. Quickly, Jeff leaned towards him knocking his drink.

"No, wait, wait. Henry, wait."

Blowing out the flame, Henry handed the paper back to him.

"And no one will know?"

"No, because it's not a bookie nor it is on a main phone line."

"When is it open?"

"Tonight. At seven o'clock."

"Should I come alone or…"

"Bring a mate if you like. But! keep it shut about it otherwise everyone will be in the shit."

"Don't worry about that. I got it. I'll keep quiet, and I'll have another."

David had become anxious as he went by as if he had to be somewhere. Henry leaned against the table watching him.

"Would you just fucking sit still; you are doing my head in."

"Get stuffed."

It was the force at the door that stopped David from moving and froze him on the spot. Henry looked at him, then at the door.

"I'll get it. Shall I?"

"Yeah, no wait."

Henry felt his shoulder violently grabbed and pulled close to David making him insecure.

"If they ask for me, I am not here. OK?"

"OK."

Pulling himself away from his frightened friend, Henry answered the door, slowly opening it just to tease David.

"I've brought a mate."

"It's Jeff!"

David remained frozen on the spot. Jeff and his mate walked in noticing that David had bitten his nail.

"I didn't know it was you, Henry?"

"If I told you, would you come?"

Henry led them over to the table and showed them the racing post. He opened the beating book and handed them paper slips from the notebook and waited for them to choose what they wanted.

"Black velvet at two o'clock. Aston racecourse ten-to-one," Jeff said as he sorted out the money while Henry filled in the book and took the slips from them.

"You?" Henry asked quickly to Jeff's mate who seemed shy, but Henry knew him very well, gay as hell.

"Oh. Yes, please, Henry. I'll have rummy at midday, 5/1, and will bet two pounds."

The man seemed pleased with himself while Henry just rolled his eyes.

"Go mad why don't ya?" Jeff said to his friend as he took his slip of paper from Henry and put it into his coat pocket.

"And don't let your wife see it for fucks sake."

"I won't."

Henry handed over the paper to the men who took it with care and glanced at them and then back at the slip, but Henry was too busy filling out the book which the man noticed.

"Come on. See you soon our kid."

"Bye, Jeff."

As they left, they could not help but notice David giving a small nervous smile as they were nearly face to face with Thomas.

"Evening, Tom!"

"Evening, Jeff. Evening, sir."

It was a relief to see people coming through the door as he closed it behind him.

David, however, would kick off if anyone looked at him.

"What's fucking wrong with him?" Thomas asked Henry as he walked past David and over to Henry.

"Christ knows? He's been like this all day."

"Here," Thomas put the ten-pound note under Henry's nose.

"Who's it for?"

"Mrs Wilson on Black thunder 2:40 five to one!"

Henry put the money in and filled the book. Thomas sat next to him watching David.

"Do you think anyone else will be comin'?" David asked as he began to become verbally violent as he went up to the windows. Not moving and watching people walk past, his face become pale as if he were going to be sick.

"It's word of mouth. Who knows? Why? You need to be somewhere else do you?"

Speculation had started to set in since David had started acting weird ever since he got with Debbie some weeks back but not knowing why; yet whatever it was, it can't be good.

The evening was slow. Mrs Wilson, Jeff and his mate bets, they decide to close the shop for the evening. Despite David protest, they made their way to the pub. Thomas slipped a note to Henry. It read, 'Got a gut feeling. David's got himself into some sort of shit'.

Henry quickly wrote his reply and slipped it into Thomas's coat pocket. It read: "Somehow, it involves the fucking Debbie."

Chapter 8
Birmingham Town

The early hours of the morning showed the cold air causing damp to form on the empty roads.

Bull's-eye had taken a poor young man down a back alley to do what he called breaking him in.

Violently forcing himself inside the boy as he pushed him up against the cold, damp brick wall. The smell of fresh paint from the graffiti was the only thing to keep the young boys' mind from what was happening, as Bulls-eye grunted like a pig while Debbie kept a look out for fear of the police or anyone else who maybe heading in their direction.

Having a 'smoke' as she called it.

The cold damp air went straight through her thin body, despite her coat only covered her top half, it was not long enough to keep her warm.

Bella had left the house in the early hour so as not to wake anybody to get some fresh air.

Wrapped up as warm as possible, she made her way into town walking past the pub.

"Bella," Debbie shouted as a warning that someone was close.

"Morning, Debbie. How are you?"

"I'm good. You?"

Bella looked at her old friends' face and could see that something was wrong, but not willing to confront her about it, she smiled and turned to start her walk home only to hear walk home only to hear Bulls-eye cry out in pleasure.

"Yeah, where you off to?"

"Just for a stroll."

"Well, it's a bit quiet round here and we wouldn't want you hurt now. Would we?"

"That's a threat or a warning?"

"Don't be stupid just go to the other way. Back home alright. For your own sake."

Bella looked at her friend's face and could see that something was wrong but not willing to confront her about it smiled and turned to start her walk home only to hear Bull's-eye cry out in pleasure.

"OH SHIT, YES!"

Bella had heard him like that before, so she knew exactly what he was doing. That made her to feel sick to her stomach. The only other thing she could think of was not home. The town the other way round.

The market was quiet; the stalls were just being set up as Bella walked around the market and the bullring.

Fish market, meat stalls, fresh bread and cakes and tea, coffee and milk that was Ernest's usual shopping list with his bruises going down and the black eye swollen also going down day by day he needed all the energy he could get from this food.

Just like Bella, he believed that he had to take care of himself as no one else will.

"Hello, you."

"Morning, Frank. How are you?"

Bella knew many of the shopkeepers despite most of the women who took an instant dislike to her, two women who own the cake and bread stall had always treated her like a daughter.

Frank knew about Ernest and what had happened to him so gave Bella extra fish for his young friend.

Different smells surrounded her as she made her way through the market with bags full of the essentials as she began to make a way home and check on Ernest.

Witton Road

Thomas and Henry had left the house. It was quite the smell of bleach she had used last night. It was strong as she went through the front door.

Bella closed the door and made her way to the living room door. The bed was folded up and neatly put on one side.

"Hello?" Bella gentle knocked on her ear near it as she could hear Ernest moving around.

"Ernest? Bella … it's Bella. I've just done some shopping for you. I'll keep them in the kitchen."

"You alone?"

"Yes, Henry's not here. He's gone out with Thomas."

The key moved in the lock.

"You OK? Coming for a cupper? Come on."

Bella remembered Ernest's flat.

Old fashioned as it was built in 1950 but spotless clean to the point that you could see yourself in everything from sink to toilet seat from which you could eat off, and yet he was here trying to avoid Henry.

While she was emptying the bags on the kitchen table, Ernest came out in his dark blue boxer shorts to see what Bella had got.

The bruising on his thin body was healing, and the sore ribs were healing, but the black eye was not so much.

"How much do I owe you?"

"Oh, don't worry about that. It's what friends do."

"Bella, come on. Fair, please."

"I said no. Now come on; let's pop the kettle on."

Ernest quickly could ran across the cold floor back into the living room looking for the wallet that he had hid down the side of the sofa.

Although it was never full of money after paying rent and other bills, he always kept some in case he needed them.

Making his way back to the kitchen, he noticed quickly. Then he folded up the bed. Henry had slept out in the hallway. They were never apart, but his love for Ernest was at times too much.

"Here. Take it, please."

Bella just smile and stacked it in her pocket as the kettle finished boiling. She made the teas as Ernest sat down.

"Here we go."

Nothing was said for a moment as Bella got out the custard creams and sat facing Ernest.

"So? How's the betting shop going?"

"It's doing well as of now. But it's too early to see how things go."

Ernest just gave a nervous shy smile and looked down to where his hands were under the table as Bella leaned her hand down to catch Ernest's eyes.

"You not going to ask?"

"Ask? What?"

Ernest' heart was pounding hard and fast as fear of what Henry had done since he locked him out.

"Henry?"

"What about Henry?"

"Oh… come on, Ernest. You not worried about him? We all know him. We also know how he feels about you. He loves you."

"Yeah, of course, he does," Ernest remark was sarcastic.

"Ernest sweetheart."

"Look, I know what he was, and I know that he loves me. I just want to make him happy, but well, look at me, Bella."

Bella got up and sat next to him as he started to cry.

"Ernest, now you listen to me. Henry loves you so much so that it's near obsession. Do you remember fella who touched your arm just to get your attention at the bar?"

"Yeah, I remember."

"Do you remember what he did?"

"Yeah, he lost it completely. I thought he was going to kill him."

"Exactly. No one would dare touch you. Henry has past a past, and there's nothing we can do about it."

Ernest couldn't get over what was being told to him. It was as if he was hearing it as though it was someone else.

"It's you. It will always be you. He's missing you so much. I can hear him crying himself to sleep out night as though he was in pain."

"I miss him fully, so truly. But I thought, by doing this, it might give him a chance to meet someone else."

"No, my darling. No. All you are doing is killing him very slowly. Very, very slowly."

Ernest looks at Bella. Her eyes locked on to his face as his red eyes sore and his face pale.

The back streets were always cold and damp, especially at this time of year.

No streetlights were strong enough to help anyone see who might be around and made it a perfect place for David to meet his supplier.

Keeping warm wasn't much of a problem. He pulled his jacket collar up and kept his hands in his trouser pocket, lurking in the shadows. It had gone midnight.

The car was a white Vauxhall, unclean, no tax or m.o.t but that was not its purpose. Bull's-eye just wanted a run around.

Getting out of the car, David stepped out of the shadows, wary at the same time as this was a man not to be trusted or crossed.

Bull's-eye greeted his new dealer, and he placed his fat hand on David bony shoulders.

"So how did you get on?"

David quickly and shakingly pulled out a wade of money at least five thousand and nervously handed it over to Bull's-eye who snatched it.

"Well done, my boy. Well done." Pocketing it, Bull's-eye patted David on the back and led him over to the car.

"I have another job for you."

David could not help but notice two men sitting in the back seats. Both were small in size, but it was not easy to tell as it was dark.

Opening the boot, Bull's-eye pulled out an old plastic carry bag and showed David what was inside. COCAINE!

"Now I want you to get your monies worth out of this lot. You understand me? You have until next week to do so, and if you deliver, great! But, if not, I will show you a very very different side of me. Understand?"

David swallowed hard as heat ran through his whole body.

"Yeah, yeah, yeah! Not a problem!"

Taking the bag from Bull's-eye, David stood still, and Bull's-eye grabbed the back of David's neck.

"Good lad, smart lad, and remember! Want my money's worth."

Bull's-eye gave out cackle of a laugh as he closed the boot and went over to show David to get into the car.

Taking deep breath, David watched as Bull's-eye pulled away and drove off into the blackness of the night and now really came to the task of dealing the drugs without anyone knowing.

It was much safer back home in his flat making sure no one could see in David pulled the curtains too and bolted the door. With such care almost as though they were hand grenades, David took the drugs out of the bag and place them on the bed. Each one had been put into small plastic bags with labels on them of how much was in each one and a price.

Removing his hat, he put them back into the carrier back and hid it on the top shelf.

"No one will ever know they are here."

Trying to convince himself as he closed the wardrobe, he removed his coat and settled in for the night and start his new job tomorrow night at the local pub. Drifting off to sleep, David really believed he had found an easy and much quicker way to make money, and this time, the others did not need to know.

Chapter 9
David's Story

Bella had got up early to make Thomas a full English breakfast since Henry had gone out at first light.

Sunday was the only day Thomas could get any time off from the butcher and betting shops.

The stairs creaked as he made his way down the stairs, still doing up the last top two buttons of his dark blue shirt and walked down the hall towards the kitchen where he could smell cooking.

"Oh, crap."

Bella looked at him as she put the bacon in the frying pan and gave a shy smile.

"I thought we could have a cooked breakfast together for a change since you don't have to work for the other thing."

"Why?"

It was like a knife stabbed her in the stomach as she put the knives and folks on the freshly washed and ironed tablecloth.

"Don't you want."

"Kettle on."

"Well? Yes?"

Pouring a cup of coffee, Thomas sat down watching Bella with suspicion.

"Why? Why would she bother? We're not a couple nor friends. She's just a lodger. That was it."

"Here, you go. I got it all fresh from your place. Hope you like it?"

"Thank you."

Sipping his tea, Bella sat next to him just looking at him as she drank her coffee making Thomas nervous.

"Alright. OK. What? What is it?"

Bella did not answer and did not see anything wrong, yet her horrified face said it loud and clear.

"Nothing."

Thomas spoke inside his head that she was lying. She had no feelings for him, but how could she? She's far too beautiful for him. There must be something.

It's driving him mad.

"Don't feel like you have to play the little wife with me, Bella."

"I'm not! I just thought."

Fuming and for no reason, Thomas voice became deep and intimating.

"When I took you in off the streets, I did it because I knew that you were better than that. I don't expect anything from you."

Bella finally felt herself overcome with anger and exhaustion.

"Of course, not. Never. But...." Bella took her hand from her cup and placed it up on Thomas's worn skin. It was warm and soft. He never moved his hand from her, and that very movement, he felt a sense of tender loving care. His heart melted, and emotions were aroused as if they had long since died.

"I'm sorry. I…."

Thomas pulled himself together and moved his hand from Bella jumping up out of his share looking confused fumbling his collar.

"Where're you goin'?"

Bella seemed surprised at Thomas reaction. It was as if she had stirred up something inside of him.

"I'm going to the café. Henry might be there."

"I'll have a cup of coffee with him. We've got something to sort out."

"But? What about your breakfast?"

"Just put 'em in a heat proof pot. I'll have it later."

Thomas turned quickly nearly falling over his chair and tumbled towards the front door throwing his coat on and fondling to get his arms in, his cap cock eyed on his head he finally fell out of the door down the step and straight down the streets.

Bella was left, stood still and confused not understanding what had just happened. She emptied the cups and went to the living room.

"Ernest?"

"Yes?"

"Do you want full English?"

The walk to the cafe in town seemed long, and the cool air helped him sort out his head but his hot blood flow seemed to crawl around inside.

Thankfully, the streets were silent as many were at the Church. Only children were playing in the streets, and the pubs were getting ready to open their doors.

"What the fuck is fucking wrong with you? Hay! All she did was touch your hand that's all. I'm so messed up. My fucking head is so fucking messed up! What are you looking at?" Thomas bellowed at some passer-by as he finally got to the cafe banging his head with the palm of his hands.

It was not as if the drugs were going anywhere and you. David still felt the urge to open up his wardrobe and look at the bundle of small packets of cocaine that each one contained.

Stood in only his vest and pants he admired what he had. The money he would earn, not just quick but at his own leisure without worrying about having to meet anyone and waiting for his money.

A smile came across his face.

"The sooner I sell all this crap, the sooner I can afford to get the fuck out of Witton Road," pulling out his blue baggy jeans and his old green and orange windbreaker jacket. He got ready for a weekend that he could sell, but also between now and next Saturday night, he would have to hunt the streets looking for those poor souls who would buy: homeless, alcoholics, prostitute, and of course the drug addicts and desperate people.

Even from a young age, David had no respect for others around him.

His mother spent more time picking up her next fella, and his dad never knew.

If that wasn't enough, it was a warm summer night and only aged seven, David had been out playing with some friends. As his mates went home as their mother's had dinner ready at the table, he went home to meet a new bloke his mother came back home with.

"David, sweetheart. This is Mitch, mummy's new friend."

The man was short and fat, bald with a dirty face who ate like a wild animal. If and when there was food on the table, he had moved in. It was only two days when young David came home from school to see a group of drunk men in the living room.

Mitch now ill-treated David. When he returned home early, Mitch dragged him holding his school uniform collar and strapped him to a heater from where David could see the living room. He started beating the young boy repeatedly over and over. He tried to protect himself by curling into a ball.

Mitch kicked in his back. He got to see his mum with men to crawl over her, so there is no point in crying out 'mummy'! She's no longer a mother.

Black-and-blue David managed to get himself lose at night and left the home for ever not to bear the cruelty anymore.

He ran away from home leaving his school jumper and tie behind. He started living in hostel putting an end to his education. Finally, at the age of sixteen, Thomas found him sleeping in the doorway of Norman's shop knowing the danger of Aston at night. Thomas pulled him to his feet.

David looked like a scared rabbit all dirty, and the clothes barely fitted him, Thomas knew he'd die out there.

"Come on, son. I won't hurt ya. I just want to help. That's all."

David walked alongside Thomas down the Witton Road, a place he had never seen before.

"In we go." Thomas led him inside to the smell of home cooking, washing hanging over the heaters and the smell of bleach. Bella made a bed ready for him.

"Would you like a bath?" Bella's voice was loving like a mother. He nodded his head. Bella went upstairs to get his bath ready. Thomas went to get him some clothes.

The water was warm, and lying there for the first time, his badly beaten wounds were not just from Mitch but also from others on the streets, and on his thin body, the pyjama was cosy. So was the bed, and yet all this kindness meant a little. It was too late; the damage was done.

Now aged twenty-eight, he refused to work and lived off handouts or money from his very small circle of friends.

Henry
Thomas
Ernest

Locking his flat door, David made his way down to the commercial staircase and cut into the car park.

The town would be quiet at the moment. Everyone either hung over or at the church or cooking Sunday roast, but his sights were set on where he was going and why.

The betting room was his by rights in his head, so he could come and go as he please as he walked up the iron staircase checking that no one was nearby. David could not get inside quickly enough.

"Why not give myself a head massage start and take the money from the bets, it makes more sense than fucking struggling."

The hunt seemed in vain.

"Where is it? Where the fuck is it?"

It was though no one had been there. Newspapers, racing paper all gone just blackboard and the table was what remained.

"Bastards… one of 'em have it with 'em. I'll kill 'em. BASTARDS!"

Chapter 10
Witton Road

Debbie had been out on the streets all night, and it was obvious from her damp clothes and frozen skin. Her beauty had now gone with the number of drinks and drugs she had used. Her poor body had been used so badly by men. All she needed now was a drug, and she had to find someone who would be willing to make a deal with her as she had very little money, and giving herself to the dealer was what she was willing to do.

It had been early four years since she showed her face down Witton Road for fear of being judged by the women there but she had no choice as the man she needed to find had plenty of drugs. David was living there somewhere, but she did not know where.

She was out of character as she never went walking through the Bullring, especially in the mess she was now in as she talked to herself. Her face become pale, her hair knotted pulled up into a bun made the customers, the public, stall keepers and shop workers stare, as whispers of what she was could be heard all around her made her anxious causing her to walk faster through the market as she started to believe that thousands upon thousands of eyes upon her, causing her head to spin and feel as though she was going mad holding her head and pulling her hair as though she was trying to tear it out she screamed.

"LEAVE ME ALONE!"

Absolute madness. She fell on the ground and crawled into a corner. She looked like a little girl crying for her mother.

"Debbie? Debbie, you alright?" A sweet soft voice. Voice of an angel as the gentle caring hands carefully took Debbie by her cut wrists and removed her hands from her ears.

"Bella?"

The sun shone from behind her old friend. Debbie saw a glow from behind Bella that she was once told as a little girl that only angels had but so had Bella from her broken skin elbows. Bella brought Debbie to feed and walked her to the nearest chair as passers-by watched on.

"What on earth is wrong with you?"

Bella had become concerned about Debbie as she had never seen her like this in all the years, she had known her.

"Nothing. Please leave me alone. I need to meet David."

"Why? Why do you need David?" Curiosity had put Bella on edge.

"I just want to. Please." Struggling to get to her feet as she was so weak and for whatever reason Debbie was looking for something, it was certainly not good.

"Look at yourself. You can barely stand."

"Please, Bella. Please help me, mum."

Bella was not the sort of person to turn her back on those in need despite their history. She knew Debbie was sick in both body and mind. As Thomas rescued her from the streets she was going to have to do the same.

Rescue Debbie. Only with one problem as to where to take her as taking her back to the house was out of the question. Thomas would go mad especially as Debbie had to deal with Bull's-eye.

"Come on, let's sort you out." Pulling Debbie to her feet by throwing her friend's arm around her neck and held her up by her waist and pulled her back up so the two former friends made their way home.

Ernest had, at last, made a full recovery from the fight. Even the black eye was much better now. Just sores; otherwise, he was fit and healthy and now wanted to get back to work, back to his friends and back to Henry.

"Ernest! You in?"

Ernest came downstairs washed and fit. He saw Bella struggling with what look like a wild woman.

"Fucking hell, Bella. Who the hell is that?"

"It's Debbie."

Ernest got hold of Debbie and dragged her into the living room as he pushed her onto the sofa.

"She can't stay here. Thomas will go mad."

"Fuck what," Thomas says. "Look at her!"

It was like looking at a mad woman as she rolled over and was sick on Bella's carpet.

"Oh no."

Bella got Debbie by her waist and pulled her back upright so she did not choke on her vomit as Ernest rubbed his head worrying what the others would say if they saw her.

"Bella, I have an idea."

"Go on."

"I'll go back to my flat."

"No."

"No listen. That way you can keep her here."

"Keep your eye on her."

Ernest gathered up his things and told Bella that Henry must know where he had gone.

Leaving the house, Ernest made his way home. From the age of five, Ernest had been dumped on his ageing grandparents who lived in Endicott Road. After his father left for Europe and his mother ran off with a new fella, the young boy would only be in the way. His grandparents were loving and understanding and cared much for their only grandchild.

But, when his grandfather died, Ernest was only twelve years old, and he was now forced to grow up quickly so he could care for his grandmother who taught him how to cook, clean, iron and generally looked after himself. Her home cooking was passed on to him, and by the time, he was sixteen, he needed to get a job as a glass collector at George's pub.

But one more sadness came into Ernest's life. His grandmother passed away but she left him thousand pounds to help him start up on his own. It would be at the age of seventeen, an eighteen-year-old boy came into his life. Henry.

Finally home, Ernest walked up the communal staircase only to find the landlady, May. His legs suddenly became weak as he stood near his flat door.

"Hello, feeling better?"

"Yes, thank you."

'Good rent'. May was a force of nature, not someone to cross as she stood there with her hand out, palm face up.

"For Christ's sake, one minute," Ernest took his key out of his cardigan pocket and went inside. The flat had not been used, Henry had not come home yet. As he took out a small, dark blue purse that belonged to his grandmother, he took out the hundreds pound and went back to see May who had not moved and inch.

"Here."

"Tar. See you next week."

Watching her go back downstairs, Ernest gave a sigh of relief. Thank god, Henry had not come home as more than once they had clashed.

When May found out that Henry was living here, she lost it. Her hatred for prostitutes was one thing, but rent boys was another.

"He will pay his way."

"Oh, yes? How? By fucking other. May stopped for a moment as she felt sick at the thought of it."

"Please, May."

"I said no."

"He only sleeps with."

"Who? Who does he fuck? That sort of creature was the reason my husband died."

It was well known that May's husband had men, mostly young rent boys. But because he was not keeping himself safe, he died at the local gentleman's club that ended up making it into the newspapers causing more grief for May.

Yet time heals, and May had learnt to accept Henry.

For now.

Witton Road

"Thomas is going to have a fight when he gets home."

Bella spoke to herself as you helped Debbie onto the sofa after cleaning off her friend's disgusting body fluids.

Debbie's eyes were black and dead like a shark! Lifeless.

"Get some sleep, my love. See you in the morning." Kissing her friend's sticky forehead, she drew the curtains only to see Thomas coming up the path.

"Oh, crap."

Running to the phone, Bella rang the pub to tell George to let Henry know that Ernest had gone back to the flat. Putting the phone down, she heard the key turn in the door.

"Here we go."

Chapter 11
Henry and David

Henry felt some peace knowing that Ernest was home safe and warm, and no one could get near him but himself, but also knew it was best to stay with Thomas. For now, Saturday night came around quicker than normal or at least that was how it felt, the bar was not excessively busy but not enough that some punters stood at the bar, crowding it, made it hard to serve others trying to get near.

George and Henry had been on their feet since opening at seven at that evening, and without Ernest to collect the empty glasses, it made them busier.

"I tell you, George. Once or maybe twice is fine, but three fucking times is a bad luck. How the fuck did that happen?"

Paul had become a regular customer not just at the pub but also at the illegal betting shop and lost often.

"I don't know, lad, ER! HENRY! Come er, our kid."

Henry handed over a pint to a regular customer. He took the money and made his way towards George who was stood at the side of the bar.

"Help out an old friend," George tapped Henry on the shoulder and went off to serve the punters.

"Go on then. You look sad. What is it?"

Paul leaned close to Henry, and Henry leaned against the flap of the bar.

"Come on, our kid. Help out an old mate."

Henry gave a small smile and looked ahead before looking back at Paul.

"Can't. You lose? That's your problem, not mine."

"Yeah, but could you? Do you know? Bend the rules a bit just! So I can get some back."

"No!"

"Henry?"

The door opened and closed slowly causing Henry to look up only to spot David making his way through the crowd.

Completely unaware of his friend being there, David was being stalked by Henry's blue eyes as Henry watched him over to a small round table near the men's toilet. Two blokes and one young woman had been sitting there for a while.

Not able to hear what they were talking about Henry saw one of the blokes get up and went to the toilet. David followed. The sheepish way in which they went really unsettled Henry.

"GEORGE. Just goin' to the bog!"

"You can use upstairs, lad, if you want it clean."

"No, that's OK. I'll use these. Also, I don't want to worry your wife."

"Go on then. But don't be long."

"Don't worry. I'm fed up with toilet sex. Won't be long."

"QUICK!"

Henry made his way through the crowded bar till he finally got to the toilets pushing the door open allowing a drunk out first before closing it quietly. He walked in to see which cubical was in use.

The one at the far end.

Using his index finger, Henry poked at it to see if it was locked.

"There's someone in here!"

David's voice came loud and clear.

Stepping back a bit, wiping his nose and knowing how the doors were, Henry lifted his left leg and with brute force kicked the cubical door open.

Quickly Henry held the door back from closing only to see who and what was going on. The lad from the table went into shock as he lifted his head to see Henry stood there. Panicked by it the lad grabbed his money from David's hands and threw the drugs onto the toilet system and tried to get out , as he fell over himself straight into Henry who pushed him off and watched as he stumbled out the toilets.

"OI! HAY! What about my fucking money? You bastard!

"I know where you live! David shouted loud enough for anyone to hear, but as he turned round, rage filled him at the thought of losing six hundred pounds. He grabbed Henry's throat and thrust him up against the wall near the wash basin.

"You stupid bastard! What do you do that for? Do you know what you just cost me? I'm goin' to fuckin' kill ya."

Heaving into the back of his throat, Henry spat into David's face causing him to let his friend's throat go. Henry full of frustration and anger leapt at David pushing his face first onto the basin and yanking his arm up his back.

"If I ever catch you dealing fuckin' cocaine in this pub again, I swear I fuckin' kill ya! Alright?"

"Get off me, you bastard!"

The door opened without either of them knowing causing Henry to push himself up off the basin and nearly went to hit David just as Paul walked in, in horror at what he was seeing.

"Pack it in!"

David was seething at the mouth with his fist still in the air. Henry never moved it as though he wanted David to hit him. It would make him feel better, but it could not hurt as much as Ernest was hurting him right now.

"Go on." Egging him on, David knew that Henry would not hit back as he put his arm down and left the toilets as quickly as he arrived.

"You alright, lad? I thought he was going to kill ya."

"Hey dare. Go on. Do whatever you need to do, but not that one! It needs cleaning if you get my meaning."

"Mmmm."

As Paul went to take a piss, Henry quickly grabbed a handful of blue hand towels and went into the toilet that David used.

Wrapping up the remainder of the drug in the blue paper, he put it inside his trouser pocket, and he used the rest of the hand towels to wipe the top of the system where it had been scattered and dumped it into the toilet and flushed it away.

The crowd were gathering to the point of overwhelming. He walked through the back behind the bar.

"Better now?"

"Yes, Ta George. WHO'S NEXT?" Henry bellowed out to wind up the roaring crowd of thirsty men and women gagging for more, and Henry and George were willing to help.

The back alleyway took the brutal attack that David gave it.

Rubbish bins was thrown into the streets and kicked down the road. Anything or anyone who was in his way he was willing to use his fists on as he feared what was going to happen to him but with a face full of anger, fear and exhaustion, David grabbed his hat and ran as though his life depended on it.

And it did.

Hands in pockets and collar up, David walked past the pub keeping in the shadows.

Chapter 12
Forced Entry

"How am I meant to explain to a man who's very good at making people disappear that you don't have his fucking money?" David spoke to himself as to what he was going to do about Bull's-eye without getting himself killed.

Too early for those who had enjoyed Saturday night and many at church, he had no other option in his mind than to go to the betting shop where there should be enough money to cover it or at least that was what he hoped for.

After all, it was his betting shop.

It did not take much kicking in with fear running through his veins and anger at what Henry had done to him. Paranoid that he was being watched, David released. A vicious attack on the door to the point that if there was anyone around, it could be heard.

"Open up, you fuckin' bastard!"

The hinges of the door came to loose as the door swung open crashing against the wall behind it.

"Fuck." He dared to go in straight away realising that someone heard David swung himself about checking for everyone who was around. "Right in and out." Fidgeting with his collar, he marched in almost storming the place. Standing in the middle of the room, he scanned the room with his dark brown eyes.

"Blackboard." Pointing at it, he walked over to it in a hot sweat.

Placing his hands on either side of the blackboard that still had the bets written on it, he took it off the wall with such force and ribbed it off the hinges and the chalk and wiped down colourful jacket. The bricks were loose. Now all he had to do was to use the crowbar to prize them out, and he knew exactly where it was kept.

Strapped under the table only to use if a punter got a bit violent, David ripped the crowbar off that was taped on. He got up from his back and stared at the bricks knowing deep down inside what he had got himself into was now out of control and he was into too deep, the only thing that drove him was what Bull's-eye would do to him if he did not have his money.

A brutal beating that he may not survive. Already lose it did not take much moving as he slammed the sharp end of the crowbar but missed it. He put his hand inside to feel around for the red box, but for a split moment, his guts rolled when he could not find it when his hand landed on it. As he slightly moved his hand over it, cold, bulk and wonderful to the touch as he pulled it out and held it in his hands turning to face the table as he examined it.

"God, there better be money inside after all this shit."

Cold-hearted cash was all he needed the only thing he had to deal with was opening it up. "Crowbar. I'll fuckin use it."

Pushing his knees on the box the first blow of the sharp and of the crowbar missed it.

"ARRR!" Roaring like a wild animal eye wide and black, raising the crowbar at an angle, he forced it between the small gap.

Silence.

Crawling off the box, David quickly flipped the lid, and there it was nearly fifty-five thousand pounds in cash. A beautiful sight!

Looking up thinking, he heard someone he emptied the tin box stuffing it all inside his coat pockets there was no way that anyone would look at him with suspicion as he moved quickly from behind the table and out of the room smashing everything up as he went as though it had been burgled.

Marching back before the town came alive and the pubs opened, he made his way home, hat pulled over his eyes, collar up and hands in trouser pockets with a smirk on his face.

"Fucking job's done."

Chapter 13
The Truth Comes Out

"Thank god, it wasn't in Bella's bed." Pulling up his trouser as Debbie laid there smiling to herself, naked on the dirty bed sheets, her hair matted and greasy fell over her head, the bed sheets wet and nearly off the bed shame fell over Thomas.

"That was worth waiting for, wasn't it? Lover."

Debbie spoke in a deep smoky voice as she watched Thomas pulled his vest on, she crawled like a dog up his torso.

"It shouldn't happen." Angry at himself for allowing it. Thomas pushed her off causing her to fall flat on her back; her eyes were grey; and her pale face showed hurt; and the feeling of filth ravaged her.

"That's not what I heard you say last night nor Saturday you screamed your fucking head off!"

"Cheap gin, Cheap gin." Thomas looked sideways directly at her.

"And a fucking whore."

It was Saturday night and alone as Bella left him the weekend to stay with Mrs Pyke. Deep down, he knew it was always Peter never causing him so much anger and pain, gin seemed to be the best thing to numb the hurt, especially after the verbal abuse he threw at her.

"Go on then! Go over to the old bags house! Fuckin' stay there. I don't give a shit! I only took you off the fucking streets!"

Tears flowed down Bella's cheeks as she gripped her bag and coat slamming the door behind her. She could no longer take any more of Thomas's mood swings.

His attitude has got worse since Debbie had come to stay and Ernest had left for fear of her being Bull's-eye's woman.

The bottle of gin had been left on the side in the kitchen unopened. As he stormed in grabbing it by its neck, he heard Debbie coming up from behind him.

"May I join you!"

Debbie was right up against his back as he could feel her breath on the back of his neck. It had been a while since he had a woman.

"Come on. Let's take this into the living room."

"Happily."

Falling onto the sofa, the pair cracked open the first, bottle then another. Their heads started spinning. Laughter filled the room as Thomas poured another. Debbie looked him up and down.

"Do you want me?"

Thomas heard her voice in his ear. It was demanding, hot upon his ear. As he sat there with a glass in one hand and bottle in the other, Debbie put hers on the floor as she allowed her hand to slowly slide down his vest and onto his trouser zip. Undoing it, he felt her hand inside his trouser causing him to groan making him drop his glass and bottle onto the sofa as he fell back allowing her to fondle him.

"Oh, yes… yes, please." His voice was slow and crackling as her hand forced him to swell as she got rough all over his dick.

"You like it like that. Don't you?"

"Yes, yes! Oh, fuck, yes please."

Removing her hand from his open zip, Debbie stripped quickly her clothes all over the floor until she was naked. Thomas was unable to move.

"Now let me see what your like inside."

Undressing him, taking his belt off and folding his trousers and pants down to his ankles, she put him inside her mouth and sucked him quickly.

His legs could not move as he put his head back, mouth open and gripped the sofa as he finally came.

Debbie pulled herself away and crawled up to him fast and sat on him as she forced Thomas up inside her and thrashed fast pushing up against him.

Screaming her mouth wide open like a flycatcher, she bands her hands on his chest. Thomas grabbed her waist hard as they cried out their heart pounding rapidly.

"Come on!"

"Oh fuck, yes!"

The sofa moved viciously fast until Debbie cried out to stop.

The drunken pair remained still for a while when she removed herself from him taking his hands and pulling him up. Thomas shuffled himself towards the staircase and finally their way upstairs.

It was only now that the reality had come to a life of what they had done was full of Bella and the only chance of them becoming a real couple was now out of reach.

Starring at Debbie as she sat legs apart, he felt disgusted.

"Get lost and put your clothes on for fuck sake."

Walking out of the room, Thomas walked down the stairs as quickly as he could. Debbie still not dressed ran for him. The front door opened, and standing before him was Bella.

"Bella?"

Nothing. No reply; just hurt in her eyes.

"No, I don't want to know."

Marching as quickly as she could towards the kitchen, Bella felt numb. The only thing to feel again was to clean as Thomas walked in with Debbie behind him infuriating him.

"Get lost!"

Bellowing at her, Debbie ran like a dog back upstairs.

It was still in his back pocket and could feel it crackles as Henry walked down the street with his fag between his thin lips only to take it to blow the smoke out. The fresh air was what he needed. Having stayed overnight at the pub not only was his head full of what David had been caught doing but also Henry could not understand why. None of it made sense.

The street was busy with people going about their day. He finally got to Thomas's house where after some years, the doorbell was working. Thank goodness for Henry who had to use his fist to get Thomas to answer the door. Bella carefully opened it to see Henry drop his fag to the ground and stamped on it.

"Thomas in?"

Weary of Henry, Bella nodded as she opened it.

"In the kitchen."

Pushing the door open, he did not even acknowledge her, just headed towards the kitchen hearing Bella close the door too.

It was as though Thomas was gazing into his cup not moving. It was obvious that something had happened, but he was dead inside not having Ernest near him. He reached into his back pocket and pulled out the hand towel and banged it on the table right under Thomas's nose.

"What is it?"

"That'll wake you up. Go on; open it." Henry braced himself for his friend's reaction.

"CRAP! Where the fuck did you get that shit from?"

Leaping up causing his chair to collapse backwards crashing to the floor, Thomas threw his hand up in the air as if he was being arrested, but Henry did not even blink just as the doorbell rang.

"David."

"David!"

"Mmm, he came to the pub Saturday night. I saw him go, to the toilet with … some bloke. So I followed and copped him dealing this crap in one of the cubicles."

Thomas put his arms back down as Henry drew closer to him.

"Why? He's got the fucking betting game. We are paying for the fucking place. OK, I mean it's a bit slow at times but? Shit?"

Henry just gave a sigh and warning look came upon his face as he looked Thomas straight in the eye.

"If he's getting this messed up crap, from whom I think he is, he's in a shit load of trouble. It's dangerous, and if he doesn't get the money they want, he will get beaten up that will almost kill him. Believe me, I've seen it."

"Bull's-eye? You mean?"

"Bull's-eye."

Thomas's guts began to roll as he rubbed the back of his head as Henry just looked at him.

"How do you know about, you know... the beatings? Is that what happened to you? You know? Your back?"

"That doesn't matter, but this... this is a big problem."

Silence came over the friends causing Thomas to sweat under his armpits.

"So what are you going to do? With this? I mean?"

The downstairs toilet was just past the kitchen and into the launderette.

Small and compact, Henry lifted the lid of the toilet and put on a pair of gloves that Thomas kept in his coat pocket in case the weather turned as it usually did, especially in Birmingham. When it snowed, it could snow up to your knees.

Pouring the contents into the toilet and flushing it, they took bath covered their mouth and noses for fear they might breathe it in. They both watched as it went down followed by the towel that had been wrapped around it.

"What about the plastic bag?"

Thomas was new to disposing of drugs which put a smile on Henry's face as he handed it to him making Thomas back off.

"I don't want it?"

"Fuckin, burn it! Here and your gloves."

"My gloves?"

"It might be covered in it."

Snatching them, Thomas left the toilet with Henry just behind him as they made their way to the back yard. Bella came in suddenly.

"Henry?"

Henry turned to look over his shoulder.

"There's someone in the living room. They want to see you."

"Who?"

Shrugging her shoulders as though she did not know. Henry pushed past her and made his way to the living room door.

Taking deep breath not knowing who was behind that door, Henry placed his hand on the front of his belt to ready himself to whip it off and use it.

Opening it quickly, Henry froze in shock as he went in.

"Ernest?" Henry's voice went soft and gentle. His eyes slowly filled up with hot tears as Ernest stood near the coffee table facing Henry, twisting the end of his cardigan as though he was scared.

"Now, don't be mad with me, Henry, please."

But Henry was not hearing him as he walked quicker than he ever had over to Ernest who refused to stop him, Henry took him by Ernest's face and passionately kissed him as Ernest threw his arms around Henry's neck to keep him there locking Henry to him.

Tears finally ran down both their cheeks. Tears of pure joy as they pulled each other's faces away just to look at one another. Henry held Ernest's face in complete love. "Don't you ever do this to me again! You nearly killed me."

"I'm sorry Henry. I'm so sorry."

They could not stop holding and kissing each other. Nothing else mattered. Not anymore. Just them. Just alone for a moment. Henry held Ernest who saw over Henrys' shoulder was Thomas stood in the doorway.

"Get a fuckin' room." Thomas laughs as he looked at two young lovers.

As they let each other go they looked at their older friend who never judged or disliked them, only ever supported and cared for them.

Wiping their faces on their arms the pair both said "sorry."

"What? Here? Now?" Henry was confused for a moment then turned to Ernest who looked a bit worried.

"Come on." Henry spoke softly as he took Ernests' hand.

A sarcastic remark from Thomas made Henry turn to look at him and then to Ernest.

"Ignore him; come on."

Holding Ernests' hand, the pair left the living room, past Thomas but not before Ernest gave Thomas a hug as a close friend. A friend. A friend that understood him and always was there for him.

"Go on, you silly bastard! And OI!"

The pair had just started up the stairs as they stopped to look at him.

"No banging on the walls!"

The pair just smiled and continued upstairs. Bella Just stood near him as he turned round only to come face to face with her very close.

"Bella? I…"

"We better leave. Give 'em some privacy. We'll go out for breakfast."

"You and me?"

"Yes, why? Is that a problem, or would you rather have Debbie?"

His guts rolled as a quick flashback came forward in his mind of what he and Debbie had done.

"No. Breakfast with you would be lovely."

The both of them got their coats and left quietly locking at the door.

The bed had not been made nor had it got clean sheets, and the smell of Thomas and Debbie lingered in the air as Ernest and Henry went inside.

Pulling the bed sheets off the bed, Henry saw the body stains on the mattress, and he touched the pillows.

"Dirty bastard. Has he never heard of buying a new fuckin bed!"

Ernest drew closer to him still holding his love hands.

"Sorry, my darling. I really am, but there's no way we are making love in that shit hole."

"But I want to because it's with you."

Henry felt himself go weak as Ernest gently kissed his neck. Henry closed his eyes as it had been too long since he had been loved by Ernest, and he just wanted to enjoy it.

Placing his cheeks next to Ernest's cheeks, Henry softly whispered, "We don't have to do this now if you don't want to."

"But I do. Just make sure it doesn't hurt please."

Henry held Ernest by wrapping his arms around his waist and gently spoke to him.

"No, it won't be. I'll be gentle; promise."

It was as though they were unwrapping gifts with such care and tenderness as they embarrassed each other.

Ernest laid down naked as Henry laid on top of him it was as though it was their first time again as they kissed, touched each other faces, their eyes, and their hands exploring each other bodies. Tears from both of them flowed down each other cheeks as Henry kissed Ernest's body. His lips were soft on him as Ernest held the pillow as he felt Henry in between his legs. Ernest gasped; his eyes closed as Henry suckled on him, caressing him and causing him to arch his back and swell.

"Hen... Henry... mmm..."

Henry held his love's waist as he pleasured him until Ernest begged him to stop as he felt himself come.

Caressing his body with his lips and laid his head on Ernest's shoulder, Ernest slipped his hand in between Henry's legs causing him to gasp, groan and fall weak upon him. As he felt him swell, Ernest spoke of Henry's ear.

"Can I have you inside me?"

"Yes."

Crawling off Ernest, Henry carefully made Ernest's legs apart and with such love and care placed himself inside Ernest who laid there. Henry leaned down to look at each other as they took their time and slowly.

Although it was slow to them, they had never been so in love than in that moment as Ernest wrapped his legs around Henry's waist.

The thrusting caused them to call out as Ernest arched his back. Both become wet and warm as Henry become hard.

"Ohh... Please."

They finally came their hearts racing, bodies hot and sweat covering them. As Henry thrashed one more time, Ernest begging him to stay there for a moment.

A moment passed between them as they looked lovingly at each other as Henry removed himself from Ernest and laid down beside his greatest love.

Grabbing the sheets from the floor, Henry took Ernest into his arms and held him tight as Ernest laid upon Henry's chest as covered them up.

"No one else is meant to see you apart from me. My love. My love."

"I love you, Henry."

"I love you. I love you so much; it hurts."

Henry kissed and stroked Ernest's thick hair one of the many features he fell in love with all them years back.

"Please, please… don't make me leave you, Henry, please."

Henry's hold tightened.

"You won't be away from me ever again. I promise. You will never leave me, and I won't let you go."

The evening seemed to roll in peacefully around came down tapping on the windowsills, and the wind whistled down the street. The young lovers slept in each other arms; their hold on one another was tight.

The fire in the living room was lit by Bella, and Thomas watched the television. At times, from the corner of his eye, he caught a quick glimpse of Bella.

"She will leave me if I carry on the way I do."

Chapter 14
Off His Head

The rain just kept coming, never letting up as it bounced off the windowsills. The temperature slowly dropped despite David putting the heaters on high forgetting about his electric bill.

Stretched out on the bed his head against the headboard his hair greasy.

Yesterday's newspaper was on the sideboard. It seemed that he had nothing else to do grabbed the paper and began to tear a piece off the corner of the pages, all the while under his bed sat a bag filled with Bull's-eye gear and why not try it see what everyone else willing to pay thousands for.

Bending down to look under his bed, David grabbed the carrier bag and plonked it on the bed each little bag containing the cocaine. He chose one that was half empty and out off his trouser pocket and pulled out his cigarette papers. He had seen everyone else do it this way. Smoking was there any other way he knew taking care to not drop any on the bed. He pinched some from the bag and with care sprinkled it in the centre of the paper fingering it so it spread out. Putting the nib inside and rolling it, he examined it for a moment not really understanding what he was doing or why, but it was too late it was all made up and ready to smoke.

Popping it between his lips, he lit up and dragged on it. The light bulb seemed bright as he laid down and dragged on it a bit, more the smoke filled the room; the smell surrounded him as his face started to change, his mind not his own and the smile of the Cheshire Cat came across his face.

"It's only right to try it before you buy it. HA! HA!"

Set around the kitchen table Thomas. Henry and now Ernest were struggling to come to terms with what David had got himself messed up in.

"DRUGS? Henry coped him in the bog at George's pub, selling it."

Ernest was in shock. He could not believe what he was hearing. It must be a misunderstanding has to be.

"Drugs Henry copped him in the bogs at the pub selling it."

Thomas just sat there calm and collected as though he was used to it. Ernest sat there in shock with Henry standing behind him.

"But? Who? How? Why? Actually, you know what? Forget it. I've got a horrible feeling who it was. Bull's-eye? How the fuck you two know something that I don't?" Thomas spoke in a sharp and angry tone of voice."

"Long story."

Ernest looked up at Henry and then back at Thomas.

"So what are we going to do?" Ernest asked with a scared look on his face.

"I don't know, our kid." It was then that Thomas stopped talking and leaned in sideways as he heard the door slam just to see a concerned-looking Bella marching up the hallway and straight into the kitchen.

"What's wrong?"

Thomas questioned Bella causing the other two to turn around.

"David's outside. He's all over the shop, and I don't think he's drunk."

They could not get up out of their chairs fast enough and headed to the front door as they opened the door. They looked up and down the street only to go white as David was leaning up against the neighbour's wall being questioned by the local bobby.

"Oh … crap. That's all we need." Thomas feared the worst as Henry walked down the last few steps gently moving Ernest aside and coldly and calmly strolled towards David.

"OI!" Henry got close to David who was now either going to pass out or be sick all over the cop. He could smell his friend. The drugs oozed out of him.

"HAY!" David pointed and laughed at Henry who just went along with it.

"HAY! Shh… sorry, cop, I mean sir."

"You know him?" The officer spoke in a deep husky voice taking down notes all the while looking up from under the brim of his helmet.

Yeah. Sadly enough. You've had one too many, haven't you, mate? I'll… um… I'll take him home.

Gripping David hard enough that he may burse him, Henry dragged him away as quickly as possible.

"Come on! Let's get your home."

Throwing David's arm around his neck, the pair staggered up the street trying to keep on the pavement and praying that the copper would fuck off. They managed to get him and himself to the garden path and up the stairs.

"Get him inside for fucks sake," Thomas's voice trembled in fear.

"Now what?" Panic setting in for poor Ernest as he turned to face Thomas whose face was white.

"Just get inside!"

Falling inside and slamming the door, all they could do now was pray that no one else saw them.

Like a ghost, Debbie crawled out of the house just as Henry and Ernest went upstairs earlier without being noticed and all because the back door was open.

The backstreet was hard to navigate. As she knew them so well, like an alley cat having her clothes hanging on her small, framed body, she crawled towards Aston Brook street. just as night fell hopeful that Bull's-eye was not back home at his flat. She could not have been more relieved to see his car gone and curtains still too.

It was always a sign that he was out.

"Wonderful!" Bent over, she watched from across the road just to check that no one else was around and finally made a run for the flat door. It was unlocked, so all she had to do was to go in and clean herself and Bulls-eye would be none the wiser but as she went inside closing the door as quietly as possible, she could tell that something was wrong.

Different cold.

"Hello?"

No answer.

Walking in, she turned to look upstairs as a hand gagged her causing her to freeze in fear. Breathing deeply, she felt an arm wrap itself around her tiny waist.

"Where the fuck ... have you been?"

Bull's-eye was only in his grey-colour underwear. His pot belly was out. He smelt sweat, and his fingernails bitten down to the cracked skin.

"BELLA'S!"

He violently threw her to the hard cold floor. She had struggled to get up. As she looked up, he seemed bigger and had a face full of violence. Nowhere to run.

"Why?"

"I don't know. But I do know that they know that David is the culprit. Mmm."

Debbie was mumbling not making any sense at all, but there again she never did.

"Stop! So? There is no doubt that Henry knows that David is my dealer. No shock in it."

"Um?"

"Fuck's sake, Debbie, David is my dealer. He works for me!"

Nodding her head madly, Debbie bit her bottom lip. "Yes, yes, very much ... so yes."

Holding his head, there was no point in pulling out his hair. It was shaved off. He looked like he was going mad and making a gut groaning sound. Debbie knew she had to somehow get out with her life; otherwise, he would take it.

The stool and coffee table flew across the living room as Bull's-eye kicked it and smashed it. It was as though he felt no pain especially as he had no socks or shoes on his disgusting feet.

"But ... but ... good news."

"What?"

"Henry?"

"What about Henry?"

"He's in love deeply in love."

Bull's-eye laughed he did not believe what he was hearing.

"What? In love? Henry? You have had too much fuckin crack. Henry fucks other men I know. I taught him. He does not fall in love."

"But he has; it's with Ernest."

Bull's-eye arms were up in the air and suddenly dropped down to his sides hitting his fat flesh causing a smacking sound. He stood right over Debbie who now found herself trapped between his legs.

For years, Bull's-eye had enjoyed installing fear into his victims and did a very good job on both Henry and Bella until they finally escaped.

"Ernest?"

"Yes, yes, Ernest. I heard them having sex."

Bending down, he gripped her by the wrists and pulled her up to her feet and marched her to the door.

"You go… you go into town to the gentlemen's club and get me the man who owns it and bring him back to me. You know him. He owns the local male whore house."

"But why can't you phone him?"

Stopping to rethink, he threw Debbie at the wall causing her to spin as though she was in a washing machine only to land towards a small metal unit hitting her hard on the corner. Blood came from her temple, in pain wiggling like a worm on the floor as Bull's-eye stepped over her to get to his phone in the living room. The phone was once white now brown with dirty as it sat on a big brown unit filled with cocaine on every shelf and drawers filled with money.

Blood money.

Debbie cried as she felt her head only to pull her hand away to see blood.

"Be quiet, you stupid whore!" bellowed out as he dialled the number and fell silent for a brief moment.

"It's me. Now listen to me. I've got an update on your young male whore."

Debbie heard a voice over the speaker.

"We've found his weakness. It's called Ernest," Bull's-eye gave out a grunt as Debbie closed her eyes and tears of guilt and fear fell.

Chapter 15
Thomas' House

"Sit him down. Just sit him down," Thomas's voice was shaking, and the cool sweet ran down his back as they all walked towards the kitchen. Ernest pulled out a chair from under the table and moved towards the sink as Henry plonked David on it throwing his friends' arm off him the whole time. David could not stop laughing and pointing at his friends who could do nothing but look at him.

"How many smokes has he had? Um!" Thomas asked but he really did not want to know the answer.

"T-W-O?" David slurred his words as he saw side-to-side while Henry stood near him.

"Hay… Hay… You fuckin stink of sex."

Henry refused to answer, and Ernest looked down.

"Ohhh… You fucked him. HA! HA!"

"RIGHT! That's it."

"No, no, Henry, don't just wait. Just get rid of him," Thomas broke up a fight that could have ended badly for David even more so now that David's head was elsewhere.

"Where? Um? Where can he go other than the fuckin' graveyard!" Henry snapped as he held his arms out as David started to fall asleep, his head collapsing on Henry's hip.

There was a pause for a moment as they looked at each other never having to say a word. They could read each other like aback.

"Get him up." Thomas turned his palms upright to Henry to get David up on his feet much to Henry's dislike.

"For Christ's sake."

"Don't fuckin moan. Ernest?"

Ernest took his hands out of his cardigan pockets with a worried look on his face.

"Yeah?"

"Under the sink, there's some tea towels. Tear 'em up into strips."

Quickly turning round Ernest opened the cupboard under the sink like he was told. The small shelf had cleaning equipment everything from polish to bleach to clean much like his cupboard at home under the shelf in a grey washing-up bowl and tea towels.

Thomas asked for it.

Grabbing them in his arms, Ernest followed his friends to the staircase as he began to rip the towels up as Henry struggled to get David upstairs.

"We'll tie the stupid bastard up on the bed."

Thomas told them as they slowly got upstairs.

"Which bed?" Henry asked as he held David upright the best he could.

"We'll take him to the spare room."

"We've just."

"Shh… Ernest, shut it. We know that but he," said pointing at David.

"Doesn't need to know that."

It was not easy as David was taller than Henry so holding him about was difficult even more so as David was wobbling or over the stairs launching his head off like a lunatic. Ernest could be heard ripping up the towels as Thomas held Henry's T-shirt and pushed David by his arms so he couldn't fall backwards.

Thankfully, the bedroom was near the top of the staircase. They opened the door and went through.

"Get in. On the bed." Thomas ordered Henry who happily pushed David onto the bed.

"Strip him."

"You what?" Henry answered sharply looking straight over at Thomas with Ernest just in the doorway.

"Strip him. But! Leave his underwear on for Christ's sake."

"No fuckin chance. I start that. He's going to think I'd tried it on with him."

"Fine. We'll do it together. Fuck me. It's not like he's got anything. You haven't already seen."

"Didn't want to hear that…," Ernest answered quickly and sharply as if he finished tearing up the towels.

"Just." Thomas was becoming tired of the bickering as they started taking David's clothes of his body odour became strong so they could not lye him down quickly enough Ernest handed the strips out to Thomas and Henry who tied David up by his wrist while Ernest got his friend's ankles. It was then that he felt sick at the sight of David's toenails.

"He never heard of the clippers? He fucking stinks."

Henry looked over at Ernest was pulling a face as he finished tying David's legs up.

"No, he doesn't. You think his feet are bad to come here, my love. Smell this end."

"No tar."

Proud of his job, Thomas looked at David who was wiggling like a warm. His body rolled around as he suddenly realised what they had done, felt anger like no other and began to scream like a banshee and cry out enough that he looks like a lunatic just out of the asylum.

"We can't leave him like this. Look at him." Ernest became distressed at the sight of David acting out abnormally.

"The neighbours will hear."

"Ernest!"

"Thomas!"

"You really shouldn't have said that." Both looked over. They saw Henry clinch his right fist and gave David a look right across his face. The first one did not work so with pleasure did it again which at that time worked causing Ernest to check him.

David was out completely.

"He's fine."

Thomas waved Henry over and tapped Ernest on his back.

"Leave him. We've got a job to do."

"What job?"

"For Christ's sake… Ernest. The betting shop. Come on leaving the dick to sleep it off."

Thomas always did what he thought for the best despite what he may feel. He cared for his friends, especially young Henry who was always on a knife edge even more so when Ernest was not around if only he had the same thoughts and feelings when it came to Bella but now was not the time as they headed downstairs and grabbed their coats and cap.

Henry opened the door. The cold air walks them up as the evening began to slowly roll in it made them see their own breaths.

Taking care not to slip and slide down the steps, making sure no one was around, Ernest slid his hand into Henry's who held it tight. Thomas closed the door and kept the key under the plastic plant pot for Bella to use when she got home.

Following his friends, Thomas placed his hand on the back of Henry's neck as they made their way out of Witton Road and round the corner towards the town.

The chill went through their coats despite the more they pulled up their collars and kept their hands in pockets, Ernest's hand inside Henry's pocket. He was not letting him go. It made no difference.

"H-E-L-P!" Foaming at the mouth, eyes red, David began to feel the cold. His head clearing but the sweat and headache were too much to bear that he started to pull as much as possible on his arms so he could get himself free.

"Come on."

The front door's key turned. That made him stop and placed his chin on his chest to try to look up to face the bedroom door, hearing noises and voices that he did not recognise.

"Shit. Holy shit!" All his might did not make a bit of difference in getting his body off the bed.

"Oh, God. Oh, God."

Footstep descended up the stairs. Creaking sound on the top was a warning sign that they were close by.

Very close by.

Too dark to see, all David could saw was a figure in the doorway, just standing there, menacing not saying a word.

"Please. Please leave me alone." David felt like that seven-year-old boy again strapped to the heater years ago as the figure made its way from the doorway and flipped the light switch.

"Oh fuck."

Bull's-eye casually strolled overdressed in black. Only the yellow hooded jacket with a smiley face on the back was the bit of colour he had on him. His face was pale with a red nose now running snot went towards his mouth feeling a sense of overwhelming power over his new victim.

"It wasn't my fault. You see... I... I..."

"Shut your cake hole."

Yanking himself as much as he could away as Bull's-eye leaned down one hand on the headboard and leaning close to David's face so close that he could smell Bull's-eye breath of strong alcohol and fags.

"You owe me money."

"Bull's-eye I know, but you..."

"Where's my fucking money?"

Fear could not set in any more than it already did as Bull's-eye's eyeballs began to turn black. The white of his eyes turned red.

"I don't have it."

"You fucking liar!" A fat cracked knuckles raised above him.

"Well, then you better start telling me, why well?"

"Please..." David felt tears running through his eyes as he feared to be beaten up. Bull's-eye came nose-to-nose and gave a sickening smile showing his rotten teeth.

"I've got a better idea for you. And you'll do it because, if you don't, I'll take your fucking life. Ask your friend. Henry got him to show you his back, and you'll see just how brutal I can be."

Alleyways were normally quiet, but tonight, it seemed to be busier with the odd whore against the brick wall with some desperate bloke, making it more difficult to get past.

Henry gave a quick look around making sure that they weren't stepping over or too close to the whore he could still feel Ernest's hand in his and held it tight for fear of falling over him or being grabbed while Thomas just tipped his cap as he passed each woman.

"Evening."

Getting to the iron staircase, Henry suddenly stopped that made Ernest and Thomas to bump into him.

"What is it?"

"Shut up, Thomas," he said pointing up the staircase. They very cautiously looked up to see the door was open. With no other option, they went up the staircase not uttering a word, holding their breaths.

"Er… our kid uses this," Thomas handed Henry a metal pole which he found on the ground near the building just in case he might need it.

Letting go of Ernest, Henry held the pole tight and with one deep breath walked in only to find it empty. No one was there. A sense of pure shock; everything had been ransacked.

"What the fuck happened?" Thomas asked himself as he and Henry looked around the pole that was on the floor.

Ernest made his way towards the table.

The newspaper and betting slips were torn up and thrown all over the floor.

"I think we've been fucking robbed."

Ernest spoke softly as he threw the empty money box on the table. The hole in the wall exposed, and the crowbar had been dumped on the floor. Thomas looked on as Henry picked it up and shook it as if he was living in hope that something would drop out. Thomas's face went as white as a ghost and felt sick in his throat.

"Shit. Shit!"

Henry slammed the box on the floor causing a mighty crash, Ernest just stood there not saying a word but knew just like Henry did that this had something to do with David.

And Bull's-eye.

Chapter 16
Kidnapped

"I'm going to fuckin kill him!" Henry's anger was now beyond control as he had finally snapped, and no one was willing to control him. Following him upstairs, Thomas and Ernest prepare themselves for the brutal beating that they would just watch.

"You, bastard!"

Henry stormed into the bedroom as he turned on the light. He could see David lying there as an easy target.

"Oh, crap."

"No good wiggling. Where is it? Where's the fuckin money?"

"Get stuffed."

Not really the reply that Ernest and Thomas wanted to hear from David's mouth as it was enough to cause Henry to finally have a reason to brutally attack David even better with him not able to fight back.

Fearing death in his own home, Thomas saw it as no other choice than to throw himself onto Henry forcing him to stop and hold his friend like a wild dog. Throwing Henry back against the wall, Thomas put his arm towards Henry just in case he lost it again.

"What have you done?" Thomas asked him to tell the truth, but David Just turned his head to face the window. Silence over the room was disturbed as the doorbell rang causing David to jump out of his skin.

"I'll go. I don't want to stand here and watch a murder," Ernest said sullenly as he went downstairs leaving them to kill each other.

The doorbell just kept ringing as though it was stuck causing Thomas to lose it.

"Alright! God, I'm coming." Ernest called out as he took the latch off only to open it. Bella ran in with so much panic and fear.

"Shit, Bella, you OK?"

Bella could barely get her breath as she spoke with her hands on her waist.

"No, not really, Ernest. You're in so much danger."

Ernest's face went white and felt sick.

"Danger? What are you on about? What danger?"

"Bull's-eye. He knows. He knows about you and Henry from what I've heard. You are the perfect bait to make Henry turn up."

"Turn up for what?"

"Sweetheart, I don't know."

Ernest's heart began to pound hard and fast. Flashbacks of the man in the grey suit came before his eyes. If anyone wanted Henry, it would be him, but Henry would kill him.

"Look, Bella, I need you to do me a favour…"

"That's enough! E-N-O-U-G-H!" Thomas bawled out over David's cries as he finally managed to pull Henry off. A black eye accompanied with cut lips and a few broken teeth finally sort to David's face as well as Henry's sore fists.

A moment of silence fell until the door slammed shut, and Bella cries for Ernest not to be so stupid causing Henry to look at the door and fearing the worse ran out of the room while Thomas was left to help David, untying him and helping him to dress.

"Bella!"

"Henry! No… No… don't please."

Placing her hands in front of her, she stood between the door and Henry shaking as Ernest disappeared out of the house and down the steps.

Henry could feel the anxiety as he tried to look out the glass in the front door before looking at Bella. His eyes gave a frost stare.

"Where's he gone?"

"Henry, now don't…"

"WHERE'S HE GONE?"

His fist was covered in blood, and out of control, Henry grabbed Bella by the throat and pushed her up against the wall.

"Where's he gone?"

Thomas marched down the stairs only to see his friend choking Bella.

"Get off her! Off!"

Thomas pushed himself between them forcing Henry off Bella knowing what could happen. Now Henry was not in control.

"Where, has, who gone?"

"Ernest. He's gone. And this bitch won't say where!"

"OK, OK. Calm down."

Thomas saw tears build up in his friend's eyes, and the woman he loved showed fear for the first time.

"Bella? Darling, where is he? For fuck's sake, where's Ernest?"

"Bull's-eye. He's gone to see Bull's-eye."

Henry violently grabbed his hair in both hands so tightly that he nearly ripped it out.

"No. No!"

"Henry? I am sorry. But he wanted to go. He wanted to help."

Not hearing or refusing to hear, Henry got his coat on. With his head spinning and tears falling down his cheeks, he left the house as Thomas could see that his friend was going to make himself sick and took Henry by his arm as he opened the door.

"Don't do anything stupid. We don't know where Bull's-eye is." Slamming the door, he pulled him back inside.

"I do."

They turned to see David, and nobody spoke a word as they looked at the state of him.

"Where? Where is he then?" Thomas asked slowly and carefully not only to scare David but also to keep Henry calm.

"The railway station. New Street station. There's a new batch of weed coming in this evening worth a quarter of a million. Ernest might go there?"

"What makes you think that?"

"Coz, Thomas, that's where the drugs are always transported and where the money is waiting for him."

"Right, we've got a train to catch. Bella, you stay here. Lock all doors and windows. Don't let anyone in. Not even Debbie. No doubt she has a part to play in this."

Nodding her head, she dried her eyes. She could see the death look in Henry's wet eyes. She should have known better than to let the greatest love of his life walk into a possible death trap.

"Coats, hat. Let's go. Move."

As they left the house, Bella closed the door and double locked it. Now she was on her own. Only she could ensure her safety as no one else was going to.

The car was ready to move off as they come out of the house only to see Ernest fighting two broad blokes dragging Ernest into the back of the car.

"Get off me, you dirty bastards."

Headfirst into the back seat, the two men followed in as the car pulled away.

"No!" cried Henry in pain and tried to chase the vehicle down the road as it went away.

Henry's face filled with fear. When he squinted his eyes, tears forced back as he watched Ernest fighting for his life and he couldn't to do anything.

"ERNEST!"

Thomas ran to grab his weak friend as he saw him collapse to the ground. Holding his friend tight, he forced Henry to look at him.

"He's gone alright. He's gone."

David stood silently not saying a word. He was like a frightened animal as Henry crawled towards him throwing himself at him to a full attack, this time in the middle of the street.

The beating was causing blood to come out of the cuts on David's face and body. Thomas allowed it for a moment when he saw enough, walked up to him and pulled Henry off dragging him onto his backside.

"Come on! Come on, our kid."

Foam came from Henry's mouth as he got to his feet falling over himself almost.

"If anything happens to him, if they hurt him, I will fuckin kill you and bury you next to him!"

Standing in between them, Thomas had other ideas.

"Get the car! The keys are on top of the front wheel under the rim. Go."

"The car? You've got no tax, no M.O.T..."

"Don't start takin' the moral high ground. Now get the car."

The rain fell heavy as it hit the windows of the car as Ernest was pulled from the back seat by his arms despite using all his strength, he could not stop them.

"Get inside."

"Get off me, you fuckin' bastards!"

The door to the gentlemen's club opened smashing the paint off the walls. The colours were red and deep purples carpet, and the staircase with an oak bannister.

"HELLO, ERNEST."

Ernest was held by his arms with his mouth open like a goldfish.

"Lovely to meet you at last."

"Oh, shit. No!"

The man had a look of wealth about him. His grey outfit with long black hair was the gentleman from the street that night Henry was nearly attacked by him.

"Welcome to my gentlemen's club."

Chapter 17
The Railway Murder

The railway station was empty. No one was around. He couldn't walk any faster even if he tried. Following him, Thomas could see Henry anxious, relief all in one with David not far behind them.

"Stop, stop, stop. We can't just go marching into the station…"

"WHY! ERNEST'S IN THERE!"

"Both we don't know that. Now listen to me the both of you. We go into the station, hang around. We split up, hide in doorways anywhere, where you can't be seen."

Henry took his belt and wrapped it around his wrist, Thomas took out his old army knife from inside his coat pocket, and David took a crowbar that he had kept close to him since having dealings with Bull's-eye, which was small enough to hide but good enough to do some serious harm.

"Let's go."

Entering the station quietly, they split up and walked into the darkness of the doorways as the rain hammered down not helped by the violent winds that howled down the tracks.

The dampness could be smelt, and the cold cut through their bodies although Henry did not feel only just numb, and yet all David could do was pray that Bull's-eye would show up and soon preferable alone.

"Please show up. For God's sake, show up. Come on. Come on, you bastard."

Peaking round the corner of the doorway, there was not a soul insight.

Time seemed to go slowly now that it was coming into the late evening and yet still nothing. Thomas had a gut feeling that they had been lied to. Not having been told the full truth he finally came out of the shadows.

"Forget it, our kid! We've been fuckin stitched up!" Henry and David came out from where they had been hiding. David took his time to meet his friends out on the platform. Thomas could see the fear and anxiety in Henry as he walked towards him with belt still wrapped around his wrist.

"Don't, son. Don't do anything stupid."

But it was useless saying anything as the words were blocked out as the steam train used to greet holiday makers pulled in, and the hot smoke filled the station. It was rare to see them unless it was there for a special reason.

"I'll have him. I'll fucking have him!"

"No!"

David saw Henry storm over and froze in fear stopping still where he was. No point in running, Henry would catch him anyway.

"You lying bastard!" Swinging the belt buckle at David violently slashing him cutting his face, watching blood come from the cuts. As he hit the floor, Henry started to kick him in the stomach making David gag.

Thomas stood by just long enough until it was enough finally deciding to make his way over to them but had no choice but to run. Henry picked David up by his collar and dragged him over to the edge of the platform. Lying on his back, David's head over the edge as though he truly believed that if the train started to move.

Henry would not pull him away.

"No, HENRY! Please for fuck sake!"

"You lied to me! Do you have any idea what could be happen to him?!"

"BREAK IT UP! GET UP!"

Thomas pulled Henry off David as he wrenched David back to his feet away from the edge of the platform.

"Now," Thomas swung David around to face him as he had enough.

"You better start telling the fucking truth because, if you don't and Ernest dies, I will dig your fucking grave."

Stood between them and nowhere to run, David swallowed hard running his fingers through his greasy hair and feeling hot.

"Please. Alright, I know that… I."

"Shh." Thomas put his hand over David's mouth as he heard a man's voice.

"Bull's-eye," Henry spoke as sharply and quickly as they stood there and waited for him this time no hiding and no running.

Bull's-eye stood near the station door looking up and down the platform as though someone was meant to be meeting him, completely unaware that he was being watched. The sky had finally turned dark and black; the only lights were the lamps and the train's headlights. Steam filled the station and dampness from the water that came from the hot steam.

Wiping his nose on his yellow jacket sleeve, the movement came from the back of the station house.

"Bull's-eye." A whisper came from behind him. He turned with care. A fist hit him full onto the side of his face causing him to tumble to the ground.

Holding his face, another fist hit him full on into his face breaking his nose. He screamed as he rolled onto his back when a foot rammed itself onto his fat throat.

"Hello, lad." Thomas bent down as he spoke in a deep guttural growl as David and Henry stood over him, Henry's foot replacing Thomas's.

"Where's Ernest?"

"Please … I'm choking… please."

Bull's-eye was struggling to breathe unable to answer Thomas.

"Where is he?" Henry was beginning to lose it as Thomas pulled Henry's leg to get his foot off Bull's-eye threat. His coughing was raspy holding his throat as he crawled to get up.

"I don't know."

"You lair!"

"No, David!" Thomas went near his friend as he could see tears in his eyes that streamed down his cheeks.

Henry raised his fist with the belt buckle still attached.

"OK. OK." A moment paused.

"The gentlemen's club. In town. They took him there. You remember that place don't you. Henry."

Thomas and David looked at Henry and then back at Bull's-eye suddenly aware that something happened to Henry, and Bull's-eye played a part in it.

"That's where we go then, David? You come with me back to the car. Henry? Do whatever you need to do. Get it out of your system"

David never moved on as he stood with Henry. Thomas could sense that something was going to happen.

"No! I want to stay. I have a score to settle."

"Fair enough." Thomas shrugged his shoulders and pulled Bull's-eye up and walked him out of the station and down a back alley followed by his friends, he threw him to the ground.

"Give it to 'em, hot lads."

The attack was so brutal and unforgiving as Henry took the belt and slashed and slashed. Thomas booted Bull's-eye in the groan fully aware that he could not defend it.

Finally, David took the crowbar and punched it at Bull's-eye's head.

David's hand gripping it so tight that his knuckles turned white; fury came across his face; flashbacks of the cruelty he suffered as a child caused his crowbar to smash it hard into the Bull's-eye's head.

The smashing hit his head hard. Blood flowed out where the hits landed.

"Now, Henry. He's is all yours," Thomas whispered into Henry's ear patting him on his back as David handed Henry the blood soaked crowbar, and Henry swung it.

Bull's-eye's head was cracking and cracking until Henry plunged the crowbar into Bull's-eye's head, and the screams stopped only when the cracked bones and blood trickling down the smashed head.

He put his foot on Bull's-eye's face and yanked the crowbar out.

Bull's-eye was dead.

Chapter 18
Savage

The room was open and airy. The bed was nice and neatly made with the cleanest sheet Ernest had ever seen since his late grandmother.

"So? This is the boy who our little baby-faced Henry has fallen in love with. I am surprised." He was tall and had thin hair to his shoulders, thin black hair with a moustache under his long nose, but at least, it gave him some colour in his pale skin.

"Piss off."

"You are handsome."

Ernest stood still, away from the bed his heart bounding and his throat dry and sore. The man drew closer a bit and Ernest could feel his breath upon his face.

"I can understand what the attraction is in clothes and…." A pause for a moment as Ernest held his breath.

"Undressed."

Flickering Ernest's trouser button made him panic and hit the man's hands away.

"Don't fucking touch me."

"I bet you never said that to my Henry."

"That's different, and he stopped being your Henry some time ago."

A vile and disgusting laugh came from the man making his shoulder lift up ever so slightly.

"I remember," he slowly strolled over towards the foot of the bed stroking the bed sheets.

"When Henry was first brought to me, he was so sweet. Innocent. But! he could give you the most erotic org."

"What do you want?"

Not wanting to hear any more of what the greatest love of his life once did for a living. Despite already knowing all about it, the man never answered Ernest felt a black shadow come over the room.

The doors nearly came off Thomas's car as it was old and never really cared for, it was once his pride and joy, these days it was the drink and whores 'wait, stop'. Thomas went round the car to grab Henry before he marched off into the darkness.

The night sky no longer had stars twinkling. No moon. Only a streetlamp upon the empty streets gave little light. David stood between them.

"We go smashing the door in. We could endanger Ernest."

Thomas's voice was dim as he lowered his head and titled it slightly to the right.

"If we don't go in there now, God knows what they are doing to him." Henry's voice was raised in fear.

The gentlemen's club was never let up for fear of being noticed nor were the curtains ever pulled back, upstairs or downstairs the reality of what the people of Aston would see.

"Look, can I make a suggestion?"

Henry and Thomas went quiet as they turned around to face David who somehow had made himself taller and bigger, probably because of what he was yet to see or find inside.

"Henry, you know the man that owns it where he might keep someone like Ernest?"

"Well, yeah upstairs in one of the bedrooms. Why?"

Puzzled by his friend's remark he listened to David talk about what he always called 'Henry's people' to just walk through as he was just showing them around, Henry would go upstairs while he and Thomas would go looking for the man in the grey suit.

"No one will fall for that. They all know who we are, the Brummie boys of Aston. Two of which are gay," Henry spoke quietly sharp and concerned not for himself but for his two friends who were about to get a shock and an eye full of what went on behind the doors.

"Do we have any other choice?"

"David's right, our kid. We have no choice."

Henry with his forefinger and thumb, rubbed his eyes as he threw his arms down at his side and sighed as he turned to look at the entrance and then back to David who only wanted to get his friend back and then go on to kill the club owner.

"Fair enough. I'll go upstairs and see if I can find Ernest. If he's not there, then I will not feel sorry for what I do after that."

"And that's fair enough babs." Thomas patted him on the back as they turned back around. David stood between them as they made their way inside.

The steps were of a dark grey colour. They went towards the door. There was only a knocker, no doorbell. Thomas and David stood just behind him.

He was a bulk of a man as he opened the small sliding peephole to look through to see who it was.

"Evening." Henry spoke softly. Closing in the door, the chain could be heard clanging making David and Thomas twitchy.

As the door opened, Henry pushed past followed by his friends who were met by the smell of rose petals. Carnations on the small table leading down a corridor. Men's aftershave of the very expensive kind filled the air. Screams of joy and laughter came from the massive front room.

Henry just gave a quick glance in there to see if Ernest was there, but no luck. Thank God, Thomas and David were shocked and felt exposed by the very sight of men young and old rolling around on the floor. Some completely naked, some with red towels wrapped around their waists chasing one another up the staircase in lust or playing kisses in the room.

"I'm going upstairs."

Henry turned and just began to descend up the staircase when Thomas took his wrist.

"We wait here. But ER! Don't be too fucking long about it, alright."

Nodding, Henry went up two at a time. Thomas shuffled his coat as David looked around with his hat pulled just over an eye.

The bedrooms were alive with wild activities. Every door was open so that he could see inside the bedrooms that were filled with lust. Slowly walking past each he just nodded at a young couple running past him. The hallway was a bit too alive as David could not help but notice that he was being eyed up by a young ginger hair boy.

"You've pulled."

"Fuck off."

The young lad erotically walked slowly towards him making David back up into Thomas.

"I'm with him." No reason behind it but scared, nervous David wrapped his arms around Thomas strapping his arms to his sides and stared at him. Thomas just smiled at the young lad.

The last door at the end of the corridor was locked, but sounds could be heard from inside and of course not wanting to upset anyone. Henry took out a pocket knife and pushed it to unlock it.

Henry held the door open against the bedroom wall only to see two very young boys in bed. He said, "Sorry." Once again giving a quick nod and closing the door, he gave a wink at them.

"He's not up there," Henry called out as he made his way quickly down the stairs. David had at this point let poor Thomas go.

"Shit. OK, so where else would he keep him?" David asked with caution.

Turning to look down the dark closed hallway, Henry pushed past them, and all three followed the path. It was black; only plastic candles let the long corridor up; bright red was the office door as they finally stood up against it.

Thomas tried the handle, but it was locked. Bolted.

"All yours," Thomas gestured as Henry who lent back with so much anger and brute force smashed the door open.

"Ernest!"

There, gagged and bounded stripped to just his vest and boxer shorts, Ernest laid on his side looking hot and tired.

"Get him up," Thomas ordered as David got him to sit upright so he could untie his friend's hands as Henry took the white gag out of Ernest's mouth.

"You alright? Did they fuckin touch you? Did they hurt you?"

"No, just stripped me and tied me up. That's all. I'm OK. I don't think I was his type."

Cupping Ernest's face, Henry pulled him to him and kissed him passionately and with joy before returning to untie his ankles.

Thomas found Ernest's clothes on a single bed.

"Get your clothes on, son."

David pulled Ernest to his feet as Thomas threw his clothes at him.

"My, my. Isn't this a rare treat?"

Frozen in shock, they all turned around, and there was the man in his grey suit standing in the doorway with very little light. Only light available was the 1970s lamp on the desk.

"The Brummie boys of Aston in my office."

Beside him stood two slim young men, rough-looking almost as though they had come from a motorbike club, the ones that put Ernest into the back of Bull's-eye car.

"I never introduced myself. My name is Dorian. Pleased to meet all of you finally. Hello, beautiful boy."

Henry glared at Dorian.

"Now what?" David whispered into Henry's ear.

"Fuck it. Let's give it a bloody good go."

Thomas looked at his old army knife as Henry removed his belt and wrapped it around his wrist as David pulled out the crowbar, the one used on Bull's-eye.

Ernest looked at it for a moment

"Is that blood? Oh for…"

"Oh, shut it," David replied as he got himself ready.

Bellowing out us though he was in the army again. Thomas called out.

"Give it to 'em, hot lads!"

Henry climbed up onto the desk with Ernest following as David and Thomas stood in front of them.

The two men walked cocksure of themselves as they approached. The four friends steadied themselves as the men finally got closer.

It was more brutal than what they gave Bull's-eye.

Thomas lunged his knife at the man but missing him. Yet he continued to slash walking in a circle so the man's back was exposed to Ernest but Thomas left himself open to a gut punch, then a headlock, swinging Thomas around. Ernest grabbed a heavy salter cast iron with anger at what they did and brutally slammed it onto the man's head shouting to Thomas to mind himself.

A grumble came from the knocked-out man, as he fell to the floor nearly taking Thomas with him. He fell face first. Thomas could only see his past flash before his eyes. The body of his friend Jude caused him to go mad and turn into Hyde as he stabbed the man repeatedly in the neck and in the back. Blood spatter where Ernest was now standing as he let Thomas continue to stab the man. Blood spattering onto Thomas's face, until he finally stopped. Now covered in blood, he was breathing deeply.

David slammed the man once more as the crowbar was causing him to misaim the only thing to hit the desk using the man between him and Henry who unwrapped the belt and threw it over the head and round the man's throat buckling it up, not helped by the man trying to fight him as David sent the crowbar into the man's stomach causing him to hit the floor.

As he fell, David and Henry unleashed a brutal attack with the crowbar and boots causing blood to flow onto the carpet. Both men were dead, and the friends saw nothing but hate, no fear and the smell of blood on them.

Fearing for his life, Dorian went towards the door as all eyes laid upon him. The sound came from the corridor.

"No!" Panic struck as he saw the door swing shut.

"Debbie! Help me!" Bella and Debbie moved a heavy oak cabinet in front of the door as they could hear Dorian scream out. Debbie grabbed Bella by the arm, and the two women left as quickly as they had arrived.

Dorian got the door open with a smile; a smile on his pale face disappeared as he saw the blockade in front of him. He now found himself surrounded.

Henry stood just behind him.

Eyes upon one another, not a word spoken. With quick nods Henry threw his belt over Dorian's head wrapping it around his neck and tightened it.

"We went you on your knees!" Thomas commanded nodding to David.

"On his knees," David repeated quickly and coldly as he took the crowbar into the back of Dorian's knees making him pass in a beginning position.

"Undo his trousers, Ernest. Let's castrate the bastard."

Thomas had changed as had the others. Their words spoke with no emotion and were ice-cold.

Thomas asked, and without hesitation, Ernest bent down to undo Dorian's trousers as Dorian began to wave his arms about to try to stop him, but David hit his arms with the crowbar causing Dorian to cry out in pain.

"Undone," Ernest told his friends as he undid the button and zip pulling them down to the floor along with the deep purple lace knickers.

"Right. It's just like cutting off a pig's tail."

"Wait, wait," Ernest crawled over to grab the gag he had, had in his mouth, forcing it into Dorian's mouth, Thomas began to cut away.

"You fucking dirty bastard. YOU! Won't be using it again."

Muffled screams and howls came but could not be heard as Henry kept the belt tight as David and Ernest held his arms out in the crucifix position.

Dark thick blood slowly trickled down the thighs of Dorian as Thomas cut deeper until it finally dropped off onto the carpet. Removing the gag and shoving the dick into its owner's mouth, Dorian's eyes rolled into the back of his head as the belt was released. He collapsed to the floor but not without a blunt force from them as they belted, cut and brake every bone in Dorian's body.

Dorian was dead.

Chapter 19
Disposal

Stood over him, they just looked on as to what had just happened. Their breathings were fast and deep.

"Now what?" Ernest questioned trying to catch his breath. The window had been bolted from the outside.

"Give us your crowbar."

Henry put his belt back on and took the crowbar from David and with very little effort strolling over to the window smashed it out the glass window pane. Thomas took the bed sheet and with David's help picked up Dorian's body and dropped it onto the sheet wrapping it up.

"You and Henry go out the window first. Ernest, help me lower it out."

Henry jumped out of the window. Thankfully, it was on the ground floor, and the car was just nearby. David jumped with the help of Henry.

David too jumped in.

"Right, quick," They echoed waving Thomas and Ernest on.

The body came head first as Ernest and Thomas guided it out, watching their two friends outside handle it.

"Get his legs, David."

"Got 'em, Henry mate."

Henry just gave a smile.

Ernest jumped out and then waited to help Thomas out the windows making sure he did not cut himself.

The boot opened up with a tug by Thomas. They put the body inside it and slammed it shut.

"Er, our kid. You drive."

Henry took the car keys as Thomas took the flask from his inside coat pocket for a swing as Ernest and David got into the back seats. The engine came to life, headlights on they drove off out of the alleyway and into the main street.

The cut was always quiet at this early hour of the morning; a fine mist had slowly come in overnight like a ghost; dampness filed the air.

It was easier to stop the car away from the damp bank so to walk down the slope near the cut, pulling the body out of the boot was a race against time before rigor mortis set in.

Ernest and Thomas took hold of the legs as Henry and David grabbed the body by the shoulders and heaved it out. Blood had already soaked into the sheets.

Clambering down quickly and quietly, they stood as near to the edge as was safe so they did not go in. After a couple of swings, they threw it into the air, as it landed with mighty slams. It caused the water to ripple and spit out.

Just at that moment, silence fell. They all watched as the body plunged into the dark cold depths of the cut* and hopefully never to be discovered.

The walk up the bank was deadly. No one spoke until Ernest suddenly stopped by tapping Henry on his waist.

"What about the car? It's got blood, and all our fingerprints are all over it."

Stillness came over them as they just looked at one another.

The car park was empty far from town, and the need for petrol was easy as Thomas had at least two canisters full in the boot.

Pouring it all over the vehicle as well as to make sure none of it got on him, Thomas threw one empty canister on the roof of the car.

Henry took his T-shirt off much to Ernest's delight causing Henry to give him a wink, he took the other canister from Thomas and poured it over his T-shirt finally using his lighter setting light to it and throwing it at the car.

Standing for away, they watched flames engulfing the vehicle, and sparks flew into the air. When they turned to walk away, a mightily explosion came throwing them to the ground with force landing on their fronts. The Brummie boys landed on their sides and saw the skeleton of the car slowly being exposed. Gathering themselves together, they all decided to take the back alleyways homes.

No one spoke a word. Never looked at each other until they saw the first light of the new day. The bells of the church rang at four o'clock in the morning.

Not a soul was up as they walked up Witton Road.

"Night, lads."

"Night, Thomas!"

Descending the steps, Thomas quietly unlocked the door and closed it. He went inside silent. When he took his cap off, Bella came from the kitchen.

Her face filled with joy yet fear caught her as she started to slowly walk towards Thomas who held his arms out to her, covered in blood and the smell of petrol. It did not matter to her as she strolled into his arms.

"Thank, God, you're home," Bella said in a tender voice into Thomas's ear as he clung to her so tight as a snake would do to its prey. He closed his eyes and smelt the perfume on her just enjoying the moment.

A moment with her in his arms.

David closed the main entrance to the block of flats not caring if anyone heard as he removed his jacket and hat walking up the stairs. The neighbour was standing at the top.

"Oh good. It's you."

David got to the top forcing the neighbour back.

"David? There's blood on ya."

"I had an accident. What do you want?"

"Mm…. Someone in your flat is waiting for ya. She let herself in. Goodnight."

"Bye," David watched the neighbour go back inside her flat as he took caution walking inside.

"Debbie?" Spoken softly closing the door and bolting it, Debbie stood up in pain covered in cuts and filth.

"David … Oh, David." Tears of joy and sadness ran down her worn face. He ran to her when she fell to the floor on her knees.

Begging for forgiveness as he took her into his arms. She did not care about the blood spatter nor the smell that came from him. All she wanted was to be held.

"It's OK now, Debs. It'll be alright now. I promise I'll look after you now."

Debbie's tears ran causing her face to become wet as she rubbed her face onto his T-shirt.

"I'm sorry so so…"

"Shhh. Come on. Let's sort out your cuts yeah? Come on... come."

The flat was cold as Henry and Ernest walked inside turning on the lamp and closing the door bolted. The light showed the blood that covered them.

Ernest took his cardigan off and just froze to the stop allowing a moment to work out what they had done, and Henry walked up to him and took his jacket off only to feel a chill for the first time not because he had nothing on top but since Ernest was kidnapped.

"You alright?" Henry's voice was gentle and soft as Ernest turned shyly to look at him.

"No. Not really."

Henry took Ernest's hand in his as Ernest looked down timidly. Henry just looked at him, tears in his eyes as he spoke.

"I could have lost you tonight. Do you know that?"

"Yes."

"You mean everything. I love you so, so much. If anything happened to you, I'd just die."

"I'm sorry. I was just trying to help. That's all. I love you. And... And I don't want to lose you."

"You won't, my love. Never over my fuckin' dead body. Come here; come to me."

Henry guided Ernest's face into his neck and held each other, holding onto him so tight as Ernest did him. Kissing Ernest's thick black hair, they remained there. Just the two of them. Just for that moment before finally going to bed.

Chapter 20
The Brummie Boys Of Aston

Aston woke to the news that the body of Bull's-eye had been found in a back alleyway. His skull smashed in, and his face was beaten up beyond recognition the police could just make it out.

Just in Birmingham town centre, the gentlemen's club was raided causing those inside to be arrested if they were able to escape via the back door.

Those whose lives were normal now feared that a murderer was living nearby although Bull's-eye would not be missed.

Bella and Thomas.

Henry and Ernest.

And David and Debbie slept with the thought that those who ever tried to hurt them or those they loved would end up dead or badly beaten. Just like those already gone and those yet to follow.

The End